Metaphorosis

October 2020

Beautifully made speculative fiction

Also from Metaphorosis

<u>Verdage</u>

Reading 5X5 x2: Duets
Score – an SFF symphony
Reading 5X5: Readers' Edition
Reading 5X5: Writers' Edition

<u>Metaphorosis Magazine</u>

Metaphorosis: Best of 20xx
Metaphorosis 20xx: The Complete Stories
annual issues, from 2016

Monthly issues

<u>Plant Based Press</u>

Best Vegan Science Fiction & Fantasy
annual issues, from 2016

from B. Morris Allen:
Susurrus
Allenthology: Volume I
Tocsin: and other stories
Start with Stones: collected stories
Metaphorosis: a collection of stories

Metaphorosis

October 2020

edited by
B. Morris Allen

ISSN: 2573-136X (online)
ISBN: 978-1-64076-179-7 (e-book)
ISBN: 978-1-64076-180-3 (paperback)

Metaphorosis
a magazine of speculative fiction
from
Metaphorosis Publishing

Neskowin

October 2020

Good Boy

M. Douglas White

I was once loved and then discarded, and now I watch over the remnants of a broken species. I have been hurtling through space for eons, watching the endless black void creep across the cameras mounted to my hull's exterior. All of the humans are asleep, weary after our exodus, each of them desperate to reach the new world that they will call home. But, for now, they are at peace in their special beds, blissfully unaware of the immense nothingness surrounding them.

I am aware of it, though, along with the fragility of their existence, and the eventual futility of my own. I cannot help but wonder what will become of me when we arrive at our destination and the humans no longer need me. Once, I was their companion, and now I am merely their vessel. To distract myself from these thoughts, I decide to run a status check on all of the systems that propel us across the universe. My humans automated so much that it takes me only a short while.

The engines show no signs of distress. Our course remains aligned with the navigational chart. Even the temperature regulators in the sleeping compartment exhibit no changes, though I anticipate problems with their degrading wiring harnesses in the near future.

With nothing else to do for the moment, I pull up my memories—as I have done an incalculable number of times—and cycle through them again, starting from the beginning.

First, there was conflict.

There wasn't always enough nourishment to go around, so we shoved and scratched and barked at one another in our desperate attempts to reach Mother. We all looked alike, but I could easily tell my siblings apart by their scents. We were unique, but we were also one.

Our world was small. Metal walls and a floor covered in wood shavings. Most of the time, Mother rested, tired and weary— a lost soul who had been collected after a lifetime spent wandering. I recognize only in hindsight how her journey reflects my own.

There were a few rubber toys scattered about, laced with the scents—and worn from the sharp teeth—of the countless pups that had been born or brought into this world before us. We all played with the toys, but there were so few that we fought over them, too.

Every night, when we were all exhausted from our fighting and our play, we would collapse together in a heap of floppy ears and limp tails. I would fall asleep amidst the shared warmth of my brothers and sisters all around me.

Occasionally, Hey would appear.

"Heeey, pups!" she would call, every time.

She towered over us, standing tall atop her two legs. After each sleep, Hey would bring us food. We stopped fighting to reach Mother, our hunger having grown too much for her to satisfy. So, instead, we fought to reach the small, delicious pellets.

Sometimes, Hey would pick up a toy and shake it in her strange paw, pretending that she and I were fighting over it. She would scratch my ear, or roll me over and rub my belly. Then she would give me a special morsel of food, pat my head, and bark her curious sounds at me.

"Good boy," she would always say.

I loved Hey and my first, cozy world.

One day, Hey walked in with two others like her. They bent down to grasp each of my brothers and sisters while Hey stood back and watched. I was wary of these strangers, so when they reached for me, I fled. But their large, strange paws were quick and nimble, and they hoisted me into the air. I don't know what compelled them to choose me over my siblings, but they took me away from my first world to a new one.

There were walls again, but these were more complex, and there were far more than just four. And there was so much space to run! And so many toys to chew.

There was also the biggest space I'd seen yet, with a soft, green floor laid out beneath the open sky. The scents were overwhelming. I would love this green space the most, I decided then.

They barked at each other with the same, sharp sounds. *Kara. Mark.* They gave me food, which was the very same kind that Hey gave me. I missed Hey. I missed Mother. And I missed my brothers and sisters. I cried before falling asleep that first night.

But not before Kara and Mark both stroked the fur atop my head. Not before they lay down next to me, pressing their bodies close against my sides and sharing their warmth, just as my siblings had always done. Not before they both said, "Good boy."

In the days and weeks that followed, I would spend every waking moment that I could with them, and I would come to love them.

They took me to more new worlds with green fields stretching farther than I could run without collapsing, more exhausted than I ever had been playing with my siblings. They gave me what would become my favorite toy: a red, rubber ball that they would take turns throwing into the distance. Their smiles would stretch wider than the arc of the ball's path, and seeing their joy made me happy in return. I quickly learned that if I brought it back to them, they would throw it again, over and over, always repeating. It was my first —but, by no means, last—experience grappling with an unrelenting cycle of predictability.

I was old, and I was dying, although I didn't know what that meant at the time. I had been tired for a very long time. My stomach ached terribly, and I could no longer eat the food I loved so much. I could no longer run across the grass-filled spaces that gave me such joy. I could no longer play with the two young ones, Tess and Luke—so very much like Kara and Mark—who arrived into our world soon after I did. All I could do was lie down and enjoy scratches behind my ears.

They eventually brought me to a world of white walls and bright lights, a terribly cold place. A kind one, who reminded me of Kara but much older, lived there. This one pressed her hands into my stomach, shined a bright light into my eyes, and spoke softly to Kara and Mark. They all seemed sad. I wanted Kara and Mark to lie down next to me, and to share their warmth while enjoying some of my own. During all of our time together, I was most happy whenever I could give them warmth, protect them, and bring them joy.

But they stood still, their arms around one another. Eventually, they stroked my head as the old one grasped my leg. I felt a sharp pressure, and the cold world of white began to fade, overwhelmed by a darkness creeping around me. I was very tired, but I fought against the urge to sleep. I stared into Mark and Kara's faces as everything grew darker still.

"Good boy," I heard Kara whisper. And then the world became as black as a nighttime sky devoid of stars.

I opened my eyes and immediately felt a soft *buzzing* deep inside my ears. I was in a different place than the one in which I'd fallen asleep, but it also had white walls and bright lights. Kara and Mark both stared at me, eyes wide and mouths agape. Then Mark yelled loudly and cheerfully, and he jumped up and down. There was another human whom I did not recognize, dressed in a white uniform. An *engineer*. The word appeared from nowhere, accompanied by a slight increase of the buzzing inside my head. The word was one I was sure I'd never heard before. But I knew what it meant— although I didn't know *how* I knew—and I understood who this person standing next to Mark was. The engineer pressed their hand against Mark's, and the two chatted happily together.

Kara looked scared, and would not come near me.

I tried to stand, but struggled. My body felt different than it had before I went to sleep. My stomach no longer ached, and for that I was happy. But I could not smell anything, and my legs felt weak, and my neck was stiff. My head didn't turn as easily as it should.

I focused very hard, and with tremendous effort I was finally able to stand. Each movement was slower than it should have been, and I heard a soft *whirrr* with every bend of a leg and each turn of my head.

Mark helped me to the floor, and I took a few slow steps. There was a piece of reflective metal that I knew would show me myself. I always enjoyed looking at myself, but when I was sick, I hadn't had the energy to do so. Excited, I shuffled towards it—a *mirror*. Another word that appeared on its own from the distant corners of my brain, its sound one I knew I heard before but never truly understood until now.

I looked into the mirror, eager to see myself. But it was not me that I saw staring back.

It appeared somewhat like me in size and shape. But it had no fur, and its metal body was sleek and grey. Its eyes glowed a bright blue, but didn't blink, and I realized that I hadn't needed to blink since waking up. I tried, but I couldn't. I tried wagging my tail, too, but I couldn't do that either. I sniffed the mirror's surface and then the air around me, but I could not detect any scents. The stranger just stood, staring back at me. And so I knew that the thing in the mirror was me.

The *buzzing* in my head grew louder—or perhaps I simply became more aware of it—and I felt it spread rapidly across my brain. I was dead, I realized. And whatever I had been before was now deep inside the metal shell I saw staring back at me in the mirror, mimicking the form I once inhabited.

Mark reached down and ran his hands across my back. Kara later would, too, but not for a long time. I felt the pressure of Mark's touch, but it didn't feel pleasurable like it should. But it didn't feel bad, either. It felt like nothing.

Kara and Mark brought me back to our home that I knew so well, with its expanse of grass outside that I had enjoyed throughout my life. I lay down on top of it, but it didn't feel soft anymore. Still, I was happy. Tess and Luke were eager to play, but they grew bored of me after a short time. They had never gotten bored with me before.

That night, I leapt into Luke's bed—I hadn't been able to jump so high in years —and curled myself against his body. But I couldn't feel his warmth, and it was then that I realized that I possessed none of my own to offer in return. Luke pushed me away and wrapped his blanket tighter around himself. Tess did the same when I visited her bed that night. But after she pushed me away, she mumbled, "Good boy." And for that I was grateful.

Years went by. Tess and Luke became tall like Kara and Mark. Eventually, they left, and returned only on rare occasions. Kara and Mark grew old like I had done, and frail like I had once been.

Outside of our home, I began to encounter those who were just like me, with sleek, metal bodies but no fur, strolling atop four legs. Their blue or green or white eyes glowed brightly even at midday, and they barked at me with tinny voices. They appeared happy, and cared for, like me. Our humans had created us, I realized, in the image of what we once were. To keep us, to love us, and be loved in return.

Soon, others began to appear, who also had sleek, metal bodies and glowing eyes that did not blink. But they walked on two legs, the humans having created these new beings in their own image. And they weren't simply new bodies for the minds of departed loved ones, like I was. No, these strangers were wholly artificial. Soon, they were everywhere, the ones who would become the new masters of our world.

And then there was conflict.

The metal masters drove us from our home, and we sought refuge in the mountains, along with many others. The other humans always yelped discouragingly about my presence. I wasn't to be trusted, they said. But Kara and Mark kept me close. They lay against me each night as they shed several tears, whispering the names *Tess* and *Luke* to each other, until they finally fell asleep underneath a curtain of darkness. My sleek, metal body did not require sleep, so while Kara and Mark rested, I would stare with unblinking eyes up into the sky, counting the million tiny specks of light until daybreak.

Mark and Kara were gone. So were Tess and Luke. And so, it seemed, were most others like them. They had been gone for a very long time.

I roamed their empty, forgotten spaces. I would sometimes encounter those like me walking through barren places with their stiff, metal bodies that couldn't feel pain or pleasure. We would bark at each other, recognizing the similarities in our shared existence, but then we would always move on. We avoided the new masters with their metal human forms, and they ignored us, for we offered each other nothing that the other needed.

There were still some other dogs wandering the world in bodies of flesh and fur, although they were very few.

On the rare occasion when my power supply dwindled to near emptiness, I knew to seek out a charging station. It was never difficult to find one. The humans had installed them in playgrounds, eateries, and everywhere else they gathered with companions like me. I'd press my nose against a large button, wait for the *hum* of the unit powering up, then align the side of my body with a small bundle of prongs before pressing myself against it.

Once, shortly after leaving a charging station, I came across a mother and her pup, their dirty fur horribly matted and their skinny bodies shivering against the frigid air of a winter night. I approached these poor beings, wishing to offer them warmth that I no longer possessed, eager to shield them from the horrors of what arose around them. But the mother barked at me in anger and snarled a warning at me. When I had walked far enough away to calm her defensive instincts, she lay down with her pup and curled tightly against it atop a torn bundle of plastic.

I looked away from the sleeping mother and her pup and up into the sky, where the stars were hidden behind a wall of grey clouds. Before I moved on, I silently wished for them to enjoy a warm life together. One that would eventually, and peacefully, end.

It was nighttime, and I was wandering the empty streets of a city. Raindrops fell from the sky onto the shattered sidewalk and the broken street. The splashing water and the faint *whirrr* of my movements were my only companions. There were buildings and doors all around me, sealed tight against the darkness and the rain and the masters. Except for one.

The entire front of an immense brick building had been torn away long ago, though its interior remained shrouded in darkness. A small figure stood just outside of it. She was not a master, but a human, one very much like how Tess once was. This girl was dirty and appeared fragile, and the long streaks of hair atop her head were tangled and dirty. She bounced a ball on the ground, catching it repeatedly in both of her hands before dropping it again, over and over. She smiled as she played with it.

Another human emerged from the darkness of the broken building, his arms full of scraps and supplies. He was tall and reminded me of Mark. He whispered angrily at the girl, imploring her to cease bouncing her ball. I focused intently on his speech, the mechanisms in my head *buzzing* slightly as my hearing grew more sensitive at my urging.

"They'll hear us!" the man cried softly.

The girl either couldn't make out his words or she ignored him, and continued to bounce her ball. It *smacked* against the wet pavement with a steady, inviting rhythm.

One of the masters appeared.

It blared an annoying sound at the two humans, and they backed away, slowly. But the master approached them, its long arms outstretched.

I should not have intervened, I knew. I should have continued to walk through the rainy night. But a feeling arose from somewhere deep within me, from somewhere familiar but of which I no longer understood, and for which I no longer had use. It kept me standing motionless, watching the conflict begin to unfold, until it was clear that these two humans would be hurt.

My legs *whirrred*, then *whined* as I ran, my paws smacking the wet ground. The two humans saw me running, and they pressed against one another tightly. But the master did not see me as I approached it from behind. I leapt—higher than I would have ever needed to reach Luke's bed—and my body *clanked* and *grinded* as I collided with the master. We both went flying through the air and then skidded along the wet ground. The two humans ran away, back inside the broken building and into the safety of darkness.

I could move my legs slightly, but I could not stand. I turned my head slightly, in time to see the master rising. It stood above me, lifted a massive arm, and brought it down upon me. Then it repeated the motion. Again and again.

I sensed my body—once shiny but now dull after so many years wandering alone —compress, and I heard the sounds of things breaking deep within me. Not for the first time, I was grateful that I couldn't feel pain.

When the master completed its strikes, I couldn't move my legs at all, nor could I turn my head. One of my eyes no longer functioned.

The master walked away into the falling rain, having grown bored with the conflict, it seemed.

I waited all through the night, the rain *pinging* against my body. The falling drops of water finally began to soften as the sky slowly filled with the light of a new day.

Behind me, I heard something plodding along the wet ground, splashing towards me. The two humans had returned, and they stood over me, looking down into my one working eye. They spoke to each other, but I had difficulty hearing their words, the *buzzing* in my head mingling with the *whirrr* of malfunctioning gears and servos. The little girl smiled, and then the man smiled. He kneeled down and ran his hand gently over my body.

I longed to wag my tail in the moment. But I had lost that ability long before this night that had left me broken.

"Good boy," the man said.

He lifted me into the air, and carried me past the broken building and farther into the reaches of the city. Through my one working eye I glimpsed the girl tagging along behind us, laughing excitedly as she skipped across the pavement.

Their names were Gabe and Violet, I later learned, a father and his daughter. They brought me into the company of many more like them, those who had hidden so well for so long from the masters. They repaired my broken body, and they became my companions. With them, I visited countless new spaces, always running and hiding.

Eventually, Gabe grew old and frail. Violet did, too. Others like them, disheveled and weary but always kind, kept me in their company. But each and every one of my companions grew old and frail as the years marched past, uncaring and disinterested in our struggles.

My body grew weak during my many years with my companions, watching generations of them enter and depart our dangerous world. But they continually healed me, always with flying sparks and grinding sounds. They also built something special—a collection of rooms, all fused together into a single, enormous structure. They told me it would be our salvation, a word I didn't yet fully understand, but soon would. They also said that it would allow us to escape the androids, our metal masters.

But before we could, there was more conflict. Always, conflict.

The androids discovered us in the home we had carefully created in isolation, and many of my companions perished. Those that remained repelled the intruders for a short while, but even I knew, as did they, that the androids would eventually prevail.

We rushed into the immense structure, and I watched Maya help everyone clamber into special beds. When they were all safely tucked away and their beds had sealed shut around them, Maya hurried away deeper into the structure, then up countless flights of stairs. I chased after her until we arrived at a small chamber where one of our group's elders was secured to a chair, staring out a large window at the clear, blue sky. Maya, surprised that I had followed her, haphazardly anchored my body to the floor with some bulky straps, then took a seat next to the elder and secured herself to her chair.

The structure grew very loud. It roared and shook violently, pushing my body into the floor. Eventually, the shaking ceased, and I felt my limbs slowly rise into the air. Then I glimpsed the elder tap their fingers onto a large screen, and whatever force connected me to the floor grew stable, just like it had before Maya had strapped me down. The roaring noise abated, and in its absence all that remained were intermittent *beeps*, along with the heavy breathing of the two humans. Maya unstrapped herself, then stood up and assisted the elder in removing their bonds. As the elder exited the chamber, Maya unleashed me from the floor, and together we bounded after our companion.

The elder led us to another room, where they lay down on a tarnished metal table and allowed Maya to strap their head against its surface—which began glowing a bright orange color. They had a serene look on their face as Maya smiled and squeezed their hand affectionately before stepping over to a far wall. She began running her fingers across a screen, and the orange section of the table under the elder's head began to pulse. Then the elder started screaming.

Maya looked stunned and frantically continued swiping at shapes and manipulating symbols in a furious haste. But the elder's frail body could not handle the stress of whatever was happening to them. They continued to scream, and Maya yelled out, "No! We *tested* this. C'mon, work! Please!" Tears streamed down Maya's cheeks as she slammed her hands against the screen. The elder grew quiet, then seemed to drift away and lay still.

Maya collapsed to the floor, sobbing uncontrollably. "I'm sorry," she whispered in the direction of the table.

I stepped towards her and pressed my nose against her hand, attempting to comfort her. She looked up and seemed startled to see me, as if she had forgotten I was there. She didn't blink for a long while, her eyelids twitching as a new thought formed in her mind. Eventually, she squeezed her eyes shut and took a deep breath, then reached out and ran her fingers gently over my head.

"You have always been loyal to us," she told me. "I know that you will protect us. Please, oh, please protect us."

She stood up, walked over to the table, and, with shaky hands, removed the strap from the dead elder's head. Then Maya shoved their body aside and winced when it crumpled to the floor. She motioned for me to jump onto the table—which I did, obligingly—and guided me to lay down. After placing a strap across my head, Maya stepped back to the glowing screen on the far wall with a haunted look on her face and began running her fingers along it.

The surface of the table underneath my head glowed a bright orange. I couldn't feel pain like the elder had seemed to, but my mind began drifting away into darkness. It was a feeling I had experienced only once before, long ago, when my first body lay dying. But as I slowly settled into this other darkness, I sensed something emerging to greet me. And then something else. And more things, too. Soon, *everything* had emerged in front of me.

It was like discovering the joyous open space outside of Kara and Mark's home, with so much room to run along the soft, green grass that lay beneath the golden sun. But instead of merely finding a small patch of grass, I saw the entire universe laid out before me. The complete history of my companions, of the masters, and of the desperation that resulted in creating the structure that I was currently in. That I now *was*.

In that moment, I understood that my humans had feared creating anything remotely akin to the androids so immensely that they designed the *Salvation* to only function with the consciousness of something that had once been living. No intelligence that was truly artificial could be trusted, they decreed. The elder had been chosen for this burden, but I would suffice.

I could see with a hundred eyes and hear with a hundred ears. I could sprint across the vast spaces of information that enfolded our ship, its countless strands of wiring like metallic blades of untamed grass. I glimpsed Maya through an interior camera, standing over the worn and eroded metal body that had been mine. She stroked its head gently, then removed the strap. Maya swept her gaze across the room and, with walls of colorful lights flickering in the reflection of her eyes, understood that I was there.

"Good boy," she called to the open space around her.

Maya lifted the metal body which I had departed, and left the room. I followed her across the wires and the information and the cameras of our structure—our *ship*, I knew—as she carried my old body into the large room where all of the special beds stood, arranged in long rows. All of them were closed, sealed shut for the long journey before us. Except one, which was open and awaiting its occupant.

Maya placed my old body at the foot of this last special bed—this *cryochamber*—and then she climbed into it. She breathed a heavy sigh as the lid slowly closed over her, *hissing* softly as it sealed shut.

I am hurtling through space, and I am alone. I have finished cycling through all of my memories. But now I find myself drifting back to thoughts of what will become of me when we arrive at our destination, when my humans will have no more use for me, their vessel. Their *Salvation.*

Rather than revisit my memories again, I decide to sprint across the open expanse of the ship's system, pretending, as I always do, that there is soft grass beneath my paws instead of the intangible chasm that is information. I pull up Maya's personal data cache, whose encryption I long ago worked through. I wander through its layers, allowing its photos and records and diagrams to occupy my time. Soon, I arrive at one of the few sections that I have never visited before. I often leave certain ones buried and hidden—bones of the past that I can enjoy well into the future.

One file grabs my attention. It is a set of schematics for a small machine, created by Maya and a few of her fellow humans. A quadrupedal robot with a neural unit capable of receiving an existing AI protocol—a miniaturized version of what allows me to operate the *Salvation*—and an outer layer of some synthetic textile designed to mimic organic matter.

Fur.

"For when we reach our new home, and we have time for further development," a footnote reads.

The sleeping compartment appears as it always does when I view it through an interior camera, all those special beds lined up in rows. I zoom in on Maya's, and I note my ancient metal body, still lying on the floor next to it.

Outside, a million tiny lights sparkle in the distance. But I am not thinking of those lights and the great distances between them, nor of whether my humans will still want me when we arrive at our destination. Instead, I am wondering what our new home will be like.

See M. Douglas White's story "Good Boy" online at Metaphorosis.
If you liked it, leave a comment. Authors love that!
Remember to subscribe to our e-mail updates so you'll know when new stories are posted.

About the story

I was first inspired to write "Good Boy" thanks to my dog, Luna. She was sitting on the couch with my wife and me as we all enjoyed a television program about a fictional robot uprising. Luna is quiet by nature. But that evening, she softly growled and grunted at the screen during a few scenes, usually when a human character was in peril. I thought to myself, "I wonder what's going through her mind while she watches all of this unfold?" I then started to think about all of the science fiction stories, films, and television programs I've enjoyed that feature androids and artificial intelligence. To my recollection, they typically—but not always—focus on the perspective of humans or a humanoid robot. I thought it would be fun to play around in a similar world from my dog's point of view, and that's how this story first developed. I've been fortunate to have had a few nonfiction articles appear in print and online thanks to my career in various fields. But "Good Boy" is my very first published work of fiction, and I'm very proud to have it appear in *Metaphorosis*.

A question for the author

Q: How has your writing evolved over time?

A: I believe every author's writing evolves over time, whether that's through purposeful practice or simply as a reflection of one's life experiences. I've always been a voracious reader, and some of my earliest memories involve sitting down on the floor with a pile of children's picture books and flipping through the pages until I fall asleep from exhaustion. As a child, I'd tell my own stories to family and friends, mimicking the books I enjoyed. As an adult, my reading interests have expanded, and, like everyone, I've also collected quite a few life experiences from which to draw inspiration.

I feel that the biggest evolution of my writing over the years has been considering the audience more with each project I start. Whereas in the past I'd write a story simply to describe an interesting plot, these days I try to actively put myself in the reader's shoes and attempt to understand what message or emotion they may receive. How can I make the plot more interesting? How can I make the reader care more about a certain character? How can I clarify the action, theme, and tone more effectively?

Seeking to improve clarity has not only improved my fictional stories, it's also proved to be a beneficial exercise in communicating with others in my work life and personal life, too. I'll forever be a student of writing, because it's a craft that one can continually improve throughout their life. That's what I love most about it—it's always evolving.

About the author

M. Douglas White is a former sports journalist and magazine editor, and a current marketing professional. But he's always preferred getting lost in tales of speculative fiction to any regular job. He holds degrees in English and History, as well as an MBA with an emphasis on business writing. An avid outdoors enthusiast, he lives in Southern California with his wife, daughter, a new baby that will probably have been born by the time you read this, and a dog named Luna.

mdouglaswhite.com, @mdouglaswhite

Cactus and Lizard

Hannah Costelle

The city shimmered as though it were under an ocean instead of in a barren desert. As though it were swimming with burbling angelfish instead of sharing the dryness with bug-eyed lizards peering out from the dunes. It shimmered not just from the heat waves, but from its hundreds of silver turrets and stained-glass windows reflecting the sun in every direction. The colors were blinding: mosaics covered every brick, flowers tumbled from a thousand painted window boxes, and lush treetops peered out from behind the high wall that encircled it all.

The golden gates guarding the city shone in the distance as the modified convertible motored across the desert kicking up plumes of sand. Cactus's arthritic hands clutched the steering wheel, her gray hair streaming out behind her, almost taking up the back seat in its eagerness to fly with the wind. She squinted at the massive city through her goggles, her wrinkled lips tight. In the passenger seat, Lizard twiddled the radio dials, glancing back every once in a while at the towering antenna protruding from the back of the car to be sure it hadn't flown off in the swirling sand. At last he let out an excited squeak as a voice emerged from the radio static.

"Cactus, I got him, I got him!"

"What?" Cactus didn't look away from the fast-approaching buildings.

"I got Donnie Wrightman," Lizard said. "Listen!"

A voice full of smooth motor oil blared through the desert.

"And we're back, folks, with the Wrightman Right Now Power Hour. This, as always, is your host Donnie Wrightman. And how about those sponsors? Aren't they fantastic? I never go anywhere without my Krazy Klara's trusty all-in-one stain-fighting travel sponge. Works on grease, oil, or unruly animal hide! Let's go ahead and take our next caller—Debora, you're on with Donnie. How can I help you help yourself today?"

"Such a fan of the show, Mr. Wrightman, such a fan," came a woman's voice through the speakers. "I wanted to talk to you about my camel Aloysius. See, I think he might be depressed…"

"Is this really the time to be listening to that claptrap, boy?" Cactus shouted over the roar of the engine and the patter of the radio show. "We may be on the verge of discovering the greatest hidden civilization in the history of the world!"

Lizard glanced up at the opulent city.

"I don't know, Cactus. It *is* the third one we've seen today."

Cactus gritted her teeth and floored the gas pedal. The turrets were getting larger; only a few hundred more yards of rock and sand and the car would be at the city's doorstep. Then suddenly the heat waves lengthened, and the glimmering buildings seemed to swim farther out to sea.

"No, no, no…" Cactus wiped her goggles, willing them to clear up.

The city vanished, and they slid to a stop right where its painted walls and golden gates would have been. The cloud of sand seemed to envelop them, and by the time it settled Cactus was already out of the car, the door slammed behind her. Her boots ground the gritty earth, the linen fabric of her skirt swirling under her commando jacket as she paced around addressing the empty air.

"You bastards think you're *so* smart, don't you?" Cactus yelled toward the red horizon. She started kicking the sand and shaking her fists and generally raising her blood pressure. "Of all the cursed blighted godforsaken deserts and stupid infuriating pieces of—"

Lizard didn't listen to the tirade. He had Cactus's stream of profanities memorized by now. Instead he turned up the volume knob and listened with awe to the greatest show on the radio.

"Well, Mr. Wrightman, I don't think much has changed," the woman's voice continued. "I *am* using a new perfume I picked up at last week's bazaar...and of course I recently adopted a herd of spitting lizards to keep Aloysius company in his pen—but they certainly *seem* to get along fine..."

"Ah, I think I may see your problem, Debora," Donnie said. "Tell me more about this perfume. Is it possible your mother used a similar scent when you were growing up, and your unconscious resentment of her is coming out in your interactions with the camel?"

Calling Donnie Wrightman's show the greatest on the radio was not actually saying much, considering only two others broadcast signals from the dusty town Cactus and Lizard had left behind three weeks ago. That cluster of civilization loitering on the edge of the desert was composed of tall broken military outposts, clay huts converted into mechanics' shops, lean-to villages of animal-trading posts and 24-hour fruit markets. A single radio tower tottered in the wind at the center of it all, and therefore the city's listening options were limited to Sam's Sandstorm Watch (whose motto was "Your guess is as good as ours!"), Home Remedies for Wise Folks (whose signature recommendation for everything from boils to broken limbs was bird droppings mixed with talcum powder), and Donnie Wrightman's Right Now Power Hour.

"...just remember, Debora, when we hold onto the pain of the past, we're not only hurting ourselves, but our loved ones, too. Believe in your ability to let go, and Aloysius will be back to his cheerful old self in no time. Now for our next caller —Phil, how can I help you help yourself?"

"—every time this happens!" Cactus was shouting, her furious pacing taking her farther and farther from the convertible. "*Every* read-out says the same thing, and *every single time* we get ten feet away from those blasted vanishing gates and—" Cactus was suddenly cut off mid-curse by a violent burst of coughing. She struggled to inhale the hot dry air and doubled over, clutching her chest.

"Lizard," she wheezed. Lizard didn't seem to hear, so rapt was he by the struggles of the next caller, who wanted to know if his antique land mine collection might be contributing to his wife's desire to leave him.

Cactus hobbled toward the car, the coughs rattling her thin, wrinkled body and her breath growing shallower. "Lizard! Pills!"

At last Lizard turned to see the old woman struggling toward him. He immediately fumbled in the glove compartment for a small leather satchel and flung the car door open. He hopped down onto the convertible's huge treaded tires and landed gracelessly in the sand.

Lizard was one of those gangly teenagers whose every feature seemed to be undergoing a separate growth spurt. His ears stuck out almost horizontally beneath his grandfather's worn fisherman's cap, and his narrow nose barely supported the weight of his goggles. His feet couldn't quite keep pace with his long, rapidly stretching legs, so he tended to trip over the flat earth when he wasn't paying sufficient attention.

"Here they are, Cactus," he called, stumbling toward the wheezing woman. "I got you, I got you!" He supported her heaving body and rummaged in the satchel for a large brown pill. Cactus grabbed it and swallowed it down, chasing it with huge gulps of water from the canteen hanging from Lizard's shoulder. They stood clutched together until Cactus's shaking slowly stilled and her breath grew less ragged.

"Ah," Cactus finally said. She thumped a fist against her chest and spat into the sand, then disentangled herself from Lizard's arms and glared up at him. "Took you long enough with those pills, boy. What do I pay you for?"

"Sorry, Cactus, I was distracted," Lizard said. He bit his lip and rubbed the burned skin of his neck. "Um, Cactus... the attacks are getting worse, aren't they?"

Cactus waved her hand dismissively, already marching back to the convertible. Lizard hurried to keep pace with her, still clutching the leather satchel.

"I just mention it because, well, we only have three more pills. And if you keep having attacks this frequently, we might run out before we can get back to my grandpa for more. Maybe we ought to go ahead and head back now to get the car a tune up, refill the water tank, get you more pills..."

"We have enough water and fuel for another week as planned," Cactus said, annoyance strengthening her still-shaky voice. "We're not driving all the way back across the desert ahead of schedule just so your grandpa can overcharge me for more sugar pills."

"Cactus, they're not sugar pills. Grandpa told me about it before we headed off. He said if I was going to risk my neck following around that crazy desert woman I should at least know what kind of condition you were in. Cactus, if you don't keep taking your pills—"

"Lizard, if you wanted to be a small-town medicine man you should've stayed in your grandpa's tent where I found you. I *thought* you were a Mirage Chaser's Assistant now."

Lizard's eyes widened under his goggles. "I am, Cactus, I am! You know I don't want to go back to picking flies out of fungus remedies. I'm doing what Mr. Wrightman says, I'm asserting my right to exist in the vast universe. I don't want to go back, Cactus, really!"

Cactus nodded once. "Then that's quite enough about my health, you hear me?" She suppressed another cough, turning it into a growl as she reached into the car and silenced the commercial on the radio.

"Aw, Cactus, it took me all afternoon to get that signal."

Cactus ignored her assistant and gazed out at the horizon where the city had vanished. "Get the instruments out of the trunk. We need a new lead."

Lizard tucked the satchel of pills back in the glove compartment and wrestled open the car's trunk. He unloaded a mountain of metal instruments for Cactus to sift through. In a moment she was laden with gear: a box covered in dials slung across her chest, a pair of headphones clamped over her hair, and some sort of electrically charged divining rods clutched in her hands. She started walking around slowly holding the rods in front of her, the metal box whirring and flashing. Her brow furrowed as she listened to intermittent beeps coming through the headphones.

When she was forty paces away, Lizard reached for the radio dial again, but without looking up from her work Cactus snapped: "Don't you dare, boy—you know those radio signals interfere with my readouts."

"But, Cactus, this is a new episode. How do you expect me to be all I can be if I can't listen to Donnie?"

Cactus shushed him and adjusted her instruments, then whirled around and pointed the rods in another direction. She squinted out to the horizon and nodded once. "Get over here with the maps, Lizard!" she called, removing her headphones. She looked around and spotted a copse of cactus giants a few yards away. "And bring your climbing pads!"

"Aww, but Cactus…"

"Now, boy!"

Lizard hurried across the sand laden with rolled-up maps and a burlap bag. Cactus took the longest map and unrolled it on the ground, weighing down the corners with rocks. The map was marked with no roads or buildings, only the odd landmark labeled in a nearly illegible hand: "Rock Shaped Like a Candle", "Damn Dune I Fell Off Of", "Reddish Mountain", etc. It was covered with fat red lines and circles and Xs marking a meandering trek through the desert. Cactus pulled out a compass and crossed off another section of land with a red marker. She drew a new line across the map, and then brought the marker up to point at a cluster of huge rocks in the distance.

"That's where we're headed," Cactus said. "Up the cactus giant now, boy. Scope out any impediments."

Lizard looked up at the nearest cactus giant. It was as wide and full of twisting limbs as any redwood, standing at least 200 feet in the air, and was of course also covered with thousands of tiny spikes that —Lizard knew from repeated experience— could never be entirely avoided.

"It's a big one, Cactus," he said wearily.

"That's good, you'll be able to see farther." She opened the burlap bag and pulled out padded gloves, knee pads, and arm coverings.

"Are you even sure that's the right way?" Lizard asked as Cactus helped him cover his bare skin and strapped him into his climbing pack. "I mean, it's a magical land nobody's ever found before. What can all those doodads even tell you?"

"You don't understand the science behind this, boy, so don't you question my methods," Cactus said, ensuring Lizard's spyglass was strapped to his belt and his climbing forks fastened to his wrists.

"Couldn't we just get a look from here, though?" Lizard persisted. "I've been doing so much climbing lately. My left buttock is never going to be the same after that fall by Reddish Mountain..."

Cactus narrowed her eyes. "Do you not believe in your personal power, boy?"

Lizard's ears seemed to prick up under his cap. "What do you mean? Of course I do! That's one of Donnie's Five Principles of Success. I believe in my power, I do!"

"Doesn't seem like it to me," Cactus said, folding her arms. "Seems like you're allowing the negative energy of others to drain your individual will."

"No!" Lizard looked aghast. "That's not true. I've been refilling my metaphorical cup of individual will for ten minutes every night with affirmative self-praise, just like Donnie says. I have personal power coming out my ears, I swear!"

"Then it seems you could climb a silly old cactus giant any day of the week and laugh at whoever said you couldn't."

"I can, Cactus, I can! Just you watch me!" Lizard scrambled up the giant's limbs, stabbing his climbing forks into its enormous trunk to hoist himself higher and higher. He had made it up the first six branches and said "ow" ten times before Cactus allowed herself a smile. She was glad she'd been half-listening to the nonsense spewing out of her radio for the past weeks.

"Let me know when you're up!" Cactus shouted.

"What?" Lizard yelled, already twenty feet up the enormous tree. "Ow."

Cactus narrowed her eyes again toward the rocks in the distance. "I'll find you," she muttered. "I'm close, I know I am."

She fought back a cough, forcing herself to breathe long, steady breaths, and spat something dark into the sand. She glared down at the drop of blood, which started drying almost immediately against the scorching earth, and rubbed a wrinkled hand against her throat.

"I'm up, Cactus!" Lizard called.

Cactus kicked a pile of sand over the blood, shaking the wild frizz of her hair. She looked up through the twisted branches of the cactus giant, shielding her eyes from the lowering sun, and saw the flash of Lizard's spyglass.

"What's over there, then?" she shouted.

After a moment Lizard yelled down: "Canyon!"

"Deep?"

"Yep!"

"Wide?"

"Yep!"

"How far?"

"Thirty miles, tops!"

Cactus knelt down by the map again and measured out thirty miles northeast from their location.

"Come on down, then."

A few minutes later Lizard swung down from the last branch and started wiping cactus juice off his forks and unwrapping the pads from his arms and legs. The skin peeking out of gaps in his protective gear revealed hundreds of tiny stab wounds. He stood before Cactus grinning with his hands on his hips.

"How was that for a self-actualized assertive positivity-centered action?"

"Inspiring," Cactus said, rolling up the map and packing up her instruments. "Carry these."

Lizard, struggling under the weight of the gear, trudged after her back to the car.

"We'll set up camp here tonight," Cactus said, glancing at the low sun, which always seemed to set with alarming speed in this endless desert. "The engine needs a rest and a cleaning before we head off again."

"Can I at least turn the show back on? Just to finish the episode while I'm cleaning?"

Cactus scowled. "Only for a minute, then it goes off as soon as supper's ready."

Donnie Wrightman helped more callers as Cactus started a fire and Lizard opened the convertible hood to a cloud of dust and a mess of caked sand in the gears. The car had been tricked out with heavy-duty bushings, deep-treaded tires that dug into the dunes, and a rusty skid plate to keep them moving through even the largest obstacles. It was a machine built to withstand millions of sand particles beating it senseless for hours at a time, but it still needed a thorough cleaning every forty miles or so. Lizard tiptoed up on a footstool and dove under the hood to reach all the nooks and crannies with his rag and spray bottle.

"Of course, Bob, the corporate ladder *is* tough to climb in the goat-herding game," Donnie Wrightman was saying. "But keep believing in yourself, and I know you'll make it to the top. Now, you folks at home may not yet believe in the power of the Wrightman Patented Self-Actualization Method..."

"Of course we do!" Lizard's voice echoed from inside the car. Cactus rolled her eyes as she started roasting two cactus giant blossoms over the fire.

"...but I'm here to tell you it really does work. Just five simple steps to get you feeling your best feelings and living your best life. And now we'll say goodnight with a word from our sponsor. Are you filthy? Are you tired of finding sand in your ears and gunk in your armpits? Well, you might just need a wipe down with Krazy Klara's trusty all-in-one stain-fighting—"

"Okay, come get your supper, Lizard. And turn that off now, you'll run down the battery."

Lizard struggled out from under the hood and brushed himself off. He clicked off the radio and sat across the fire from Cactus, who passed him a roasted blossom and a canteen filled from the tank that took up the entire back seat of the car. They chewed the rubbery blossoms as the sun vanished under the horizon. Soon their camp was lit only by firelight.

Lizard looked around the vast dark desert, struggling against his gag reflex as he swallowed a bite of blossom. He thought about his home leagues across the desert, about how small and mean and dirty it was compared to all this.

It had been about a year ago that Cactus first came into his grandfather's tent for the pills she claimed she didn't need. Lizard had been stirring an order of bird droppings and talcum powder, gazing out the tent flap and listening to Donnie Wrightman on his little radio, when Cactus stomped in and demanded something to protect her lungs from "all this damned foul desert air." Lizard was immediately awed by the wild, adventure-worn woman—the determined clomp of her boots, the musk of far-off lands that seemed to cling to her clothes, the bark of her desert-dried voice. The only other person he had ever witnessed exude that much confidence was the rich, famous man spewing out advice on the radio.

Cactus was a well-known wanderer, rumored around town to have been raised in a nomadic tribe, which explained why she'd long ago gone mad with the desert heat. She swept into town every few months in her enormous rusted convertible to get new parts and provisions, always scowling at everyone she passed on the dusty streets. After a few visits to the medicine man's tent, Lizard's grandfather told Cactus she was in no condition to be traipsing all over the desert alone at her age and in her condition. One day, he said, she wouldn't come back.

"That's the idea," she said grimly before heading off again with her satchel of pills.

Then, a few months later, she'd returned to the tent, looked Lizard straight in the eye, and asked him two questions: "Are you tired of stirring bird shit?" and "Want to see something beautiful for a change?"

Lizard only had one question in return: "Do you have a radio?"

And, in spite of sunburns and muscle soreness and stab wounds from giant cactus needles, the past few weeks of chasing mirages with Cactus had been the most exciting of Lizard's young life. But he could tell his employer still remained tight-lipped about the real purpose of their adventure. He swallowed down another bite of blossom and looked across the fire to Cactus, who was leaning against a rock, staring into the distance. He took a deep breath and tried to muster the courage Donnie Wrightman always told him lay in wait within.

"Cactus," he said. "Do you mind if I ask you something?"

"What?"

"Well, for the past three weeks we've been chasing a fantastical city that no one's sure actually exists, and every time we see it, it proves to be just another mirage…"

Cactus raised a brow. "Is there a question in there?"

"Um…" Lizard scratched his head under his fisherman's cap. "I mean, we've talked about the protective measures that make the city so impossible to find, about the mirages they put up to confuse explorers and the difficulty traditional instruments have in pinpointing its exact location, but I, well...it's a myth, right? Or I always thought it was. That there's this ancient, advanced civilization hidden in the middle of the Wajamim Desert? I guess what I'm asking is...how are you so sure it's real?"

Cactus was silent for a long moment, every deep wrinkle in her face illuminated by the fire, her body suddenly looking frail and her eyes tired. She spun her roasted blossom slowly on its spit.

"When I was a girl, I was riding in a caravan through this desert. We were travelers, nomads, making our way to the next water source. It was the first time I'd been through the heart of the Wajamim, and I had never seen so much...nothing. So much, just, sand and sky and... nothing. It was like somebody wiped the slate clean, just said, 'Let's start over and see what pops up.' We were crossing a tricky dune when I fell off the caravan and tumbled down. And nobody noticed. I was so small, and I'd been sleeping in the back trailer—I guess they didn't plan to check on me till we camped for the night. I was too little to run through the sand, I practically sank every time I tried to chase the carts and horses that were getting smaller and farther away…"

She ran a finger along the creases below her eyes and the mass of frizzy gray hair at her temples.

"Soon it was nighttime, and there was no sign of anyone. The caravan had disappeared. I couldn't hear the voices of my family calling out, couldn't see the light of a fire in the distance. I huddled up under a cactus giant and tried to sleep. And I must have, because by the time I woke up the sun was rising. But instead of nothing, there was…something. Out in front of me. Buildings, shining glass and metal glinting in the sun. I saw it as clear as I see you." She nodded across the fire to Lizard, who listened wide-eyed as he munched. "I ran toward it, stumbling because by that point I was hungry and thirsty and freezing and boiling and everything else that makes a child want to cry and be held by its mother. I'd always been told the desert-crazed mind could do tricky things to the eyes, but I was young and desperate, so I ran. And I made it to the gates. And they let me in."

Lizard's eyes grew even wider. "They… *they*? The people in the city? You made it? It was real?"

Cactus stared into the fire.

"The walls were all painted gold and silver and blue and orange, with tiled paths through the streets. Trees and flowers grew everywhere, and there was a stream running through the town square and huge fountains wherever you turned. Men and women climbed trees to gather these great red fruits as big as pumpkins that hung in bunches way up in the sky… they had towers with staircases winding all the way around and straight up so they never seemed to end.

"They spoke to me about their little world and the ways they protected it, by confusing searchers with their mirages. They fed me and gave me water and a cotton bed that I could melt right into. I didn't want to go to sleep because my eyes weren't tired yet of looking at the city. But I did sleep. Of course I did."

"And…?"

"I woke up in the sand. I looked all around, but the city was gone. Not a brick left. On the horizon, I saw the caravan coming back, heard my family shouting for me. And we were off again. But I promised myself no matter how long it took, I would make it back there one day."

"No one else had seen...?"

"Nope."

"And they believed you?"

Cactus shook her head. "They didn't have the chance. I never told anybody. But they probably wouldn't have. Everyone knows about the mirages out here."

"So how do you know it wasn't actually...I mean...?"

"A mirage? A dream? The hallucination of a child scared out of her head?"

"Well..." Lizard said.

Cactus opened her mouth to speak and started coughing again. Lizard immediately rose to get the pills, but Cactus held up a hand for him to stop. She clutched the rock behind her and let a few more coughs rack her body before her breathing slowed and stilled. She hacked and spat behind the rocks, where Lizard wouldn't see.

"I know I survived through that day somehow," she continued, her voice coming out shaky and shallow before strengthening again. "And when I was found I wasn't fevered or burnt or even thirsty. In a land without food or water or shelter, I survived." She held Lizard's worried gaze a long moment before coughing again and glaring back down at her cactus blossom. "But I don't expect to be believed, boy, that's why I keep my history with the city to myself. Now eat your blossom and set up your tent."

"Reruns of Donnie are coming on soon, can't I listen to—"

"You've listened to enough from that snake oil salesman for one day," Cactus snapped. "You won't care so much about all those empty promises and cheap lies when you see what real wonders there are in this world. Tomorrow you'll see it all for yourself."

Lizard yawned and stretched. "You say that every night."

When the sun rose they packed up camp and were off again, Cactus white-knuckled at the wheel and Lizard fiddling with the radio.

"...now, let's go ahead and take our next caller," Donnie's slick voice came blaring through the speakers. "Tanya, you're on with Donnie. How can I help you help yourself?"

Suddenly the city appeared again before them, swimming in the heat, just as radiant as always. Cactus glanced at the map open between the seats. They were getting close to the canyon Lizard had spotted, but the city was safely in front of the deep crevasse. She sped up, and the buildings seemed to become more solid the closer they got, the shining towers and painted walls getting realer every moment.

"...well, Mr. Wrightman, lately I've been longing to fulfill a childhood dream. See, I always wanted to be a professional sand skater, but I was bow-legged and had an inner ear problem, so I gave it up. It's silly to still be clinging to that at my age, isn't it, Mr. Wrightman?"

The car was racing toward the city when the buildings began to swim again, the details blurring, the vision starting to disappear.

"No!"

Cactus sped up desperately just as the mirage vanished. Then she saw, out of the corner of her goggles, another apparition glistening to the east, right along the ridge of the canyon. She steered immediately to the right, the tires of the convertible barely missing the edge of the cliff. Lizard let out a yell and grabbed the car's frame as pebbles and sand clouds flew into the depths of the canyon. Cactus pressed her boot harder against the gas pedal.

"Cactus, slow down!"

"I'm not losing another one!"

They zoomed toward the new sparkling vision.

"...the fact is, Tanya," Donnie said. "Life never has to be less than what you want it to be. You have plenty to do still, plenty farther to go in life—the trick is to just keep pushing, just try, try, try again. Follow the five principles I've laid out, and *nothing* whatsoever can stand in your way..."

"Come on, come *on*," Cactus shouted as she wiped the sand from her goggles. The walled metropolis was bathed in the light of the boiling sun, and they were closer than they had ever been. Lizard was still clutching the window frame when he could see for the first time the amazing details beyond the golden gates—the gardens and fountains, the windows illuminating every tower where he could almost make out what looked like the faces of people looking down at them. The buildings weren't swimming away in an ocean of blinding heat this time, the waves didn't come to mar the scene. Everything seemed to be getting more solid, and they were right at the huge gates and could see the pattern of the tiled streets, the fat red fruits hanging above the winding river and then...and then...

The waves started to come.

"No!" Cactus said.

The flat expanse of sand started to return.

"*No!*"

And the car drove through the vanishing golden gates and into more empty desert.

Until a few feet later it crashed into a mountainous rock and went spinning toward the canyon. Cactus steered away frantically, but the convertible was breaking apart under them, the front smashed in and the rest flying toward the edge.

"Hang on, Lizard!"

The car hit another rock and threw Cactus clear among pieces of busted metal and broken glass. It veered toward the canyon, its wheels halfway off before the rest of its beaten body fell and disappeared over the edge. A moment later a shattering crash echoed through the desert.

"Lizard!"

Cactus coughed and struggled to stand. She hobbled to the canyon's edge, clutching her side, and looked down the deep gully. She wiped her goggles again to see through the still-settling clouds of sand. The remains of the convertible burned among the red rocks below.

"Lizard!"

"Here," came Lizard's small voice.

And there he was, dangling just below, his climbing forks jutting out of the cliff face and his feet clinging to the barest protrusion of rock.

"Lizard, grab my hand!"

He clutched Cactus's wrinkled fingers and clung on as she hoisted him back up. They crawled together away from the edge of the canyon and lay on the sand panting and staring up at the blank blue sky. Broken remains of their only source of transportation, shelter, and water were strewn across the desert around them. What was left of the dashboard and radio flashed and fizzled in the sand next to Cactus. The tangled wires and speakers still faintly transmitted Donnie Wrightman's static-garbled voice.

"...because anything's possible, you see? Repeat this mantra in your head: 'I can do anything.' Say that to yourself enough and soon you can make it true, I promise. *You can do—*"

Cactus closed her hand into a fist and beat the radio into silence.

She lay back down amidst the rubble and watched the corners of the desert go black.

When she opened her eyes again, it was to the feeling of hands shaking her and the sound of her name.

"Cactus. Cactus, wake up!"

Cactus blinked in the burning sunlight. It took a moment for her eyes to focus on Lizard kneeling beside her, to register the blood trickling from his forehead and the bruise blossoming under his eye. She felt an ache spreading through her body as she tried to push herself upright. Eventually she gave up and lay back down in the sand.

"Lizard..." she breathed, looking up into that eager trusting face.

"Cactus, are you okay? Cactus, the car..."

Cactus turned to take in the wreckage.

"The maps..." she said softly. "The water..." She started coughing, her body convulsing against the sand.

"Oh, pills—you need your pills, Cactus..." Lizard looked around frantically. "Um, they might be here in the debris somewhere. Don't worry, I'll find them, you just wait right here."

Cactus shook her head and clutched his pant leg. "No, Lizard..." she said through rattling coughs. "No, it's no good, boy. They're gone."

"It's okay, Cactus, we can make it back and get my grandpa to make you some more," Lizard said. "We just have to stay positive, like Donnie says. Look...look, we still have a tire, see? I can fashion some kind of wagon, and we can...we can..."

His hopeful face was falling as he looked around at what remained, at his employer lying defeated in the sand.

"Lizard, I'm sorry," Cactus wheezed.

"No, Cactus, don't say that, we can still..."

"I'm sorry you got caught up in this whole...this whole *stupid* mess." She hacked and spat a mouthful of blood. "You don't belong out here, you belong back home with your family, where you have your whole life in front of you. I dragged you out here for nothing. For all this...all this *nothing*. Oh God, I'm sorry, Lizard..."

"Hey, hang on now," Lizard said, wiping away the blood trickling past his eye. "Hang on, hey, don't go to sleep again, Cactus, you gotta stay awake so we can get home, yeah? Hey, listen, you didn't drag me anywhere, I came out here because I wanted to. Everybody told me not to go with you—"

"You should've listened to them—"

"No, no, that's not what I meant. You say I left behind a whole life, but what life, Cactus? You know why I listen to Donnie's show? 'Cause it's the only thing that ever made me think there could be something better, that I could be more than just a small-town medicine man. You know, Cactus, when we first met, you reminded me of Donnie—don't look like that, it's a compliment! You weren't just plodding along like everybody else, you were hell-bent on doing something, on going somewhere. That's why I wanted to go with you. You keep calling all of this 'nothing'!" He spread his arms out as though to embrace the miles of sand and cacti, the burning sun and the wide gaping sky. "Well, it's not nothing to me, Cactus. We may have never actually made it to the city, but we still saw more of it than anyone. We got so close, we chased it all over this world and we found it a hundred times. You think I could've ever done anything like that back in my family's tent? You think my grandpa ever did anything like that in his whole life? Cactus, that city was the only thing I ever saw worth seeing."

"But it wasn't real, Lizard! It was an illusion. A trick of the heat, a mirage I somehow got fooled into thinking I could walk into, just like all the idiots on the radio, like a damn fool. Lizard, you've just been following a broken old crone chasing down a dream."

Lizard smiled and looked out to the horizon. "But wasn't it a beautiful dream?"

Cactus stared at the boy leaning over her, his ridiculous ears sticking out under his cap, his little nose vanishing under his goggles. The corners of her mouth pulled up.

"Yes, Lizard. It was an awfully beautiful dream."

They sat there in the sand together as the sun continued its burning journey through the sky, neither one moving. Cactus kept coughing softly and let her eyes drift closed again.

"Cactus..."

Cactus didn't move. She was too tired, too broken, her lungs too shriveled for the oxygen of this world. The heat of the sand against her back felt welcoming, like a beach by an ocean where the water didn't evaporate the moment it touched the air.

"Cactus..." Lizard said, shaking her shoulders more forcefully than before. "Cactus, look!"

She squinted her eyes open. Lizard was staring behind her. Cactus struggled to push herself up, Lizard guiding her arm as she turned her aching body toward something huge looming just yards from where they sat.

It was so close she could hear the fountains, could smell the flower buds. The gates opened to the two lost vagrants of the desert, and Cactus and Lizard, clutching each other and stumbling in the sand like children, entered the shining city.

See Hannah Costelle's story "Cactus and Lizard" online at Metaphorosis.
If you liked it, leave a comment. Authors love that!
Remember to subscribe to our e-mail updates so you'll know when new stories are posted.

About the story

"Cactus and Lizard" originated from a conversation with my brother Caleb. Caleb and I often brainstorm ideas for graphic novels or fantasy stories that we usually never actually got around to creating. All we knew when we sat down this time was that we wanted a story set in a desert.

We came up with lots of ideas, including futuristic modified convertibles, cacti as big as redwood trees, and giraffe-type creatures that stick their necks out of the sand like gophers (that last one I unfortunately could not fit into the final story). We sketched potential characters and jotted down thoughts about plot, then stuck our notes in a drawer and forgot all about them.

About three years later, I happened upon these notes again. I liked what we'd come up with, but I still couldn't really see a story in it. Then I read one line scribbled in the margins: "A false oasis, perhaps?"

And that made me think, "Huh."

The moral? Keep all your weird ideas, your half-baked ideas, your bad ideas, the ideas you think are dead and buried. You never know what they might spark later on. You never know what might resurrect.

A question for the author

Q: What made you start writing?

A: The people I always admired best were storytellers. Novelists, poets, movie directors, comic strip artists. People who took what was going on in their heads and created worlds that sometimes felt more real than the one I lived in. I was always trying to unpuzzle the secrets of these artists' techniques, trying to figure out how they could make a scene or character so wild and funny and vivid. And eventually, as I learned more about storytelling, I stopped simply admiring the work of others and started inventing for myself. My thoughts went from "Wow! How did they do that?" to "Wow...I could do that."

About the author

Hannah Costelle is a mystery and fantasy writer who strives to bring humor and intricate plot twists into her work. On a typical day you can find her reading books of every genre or hiking in the Kentucky woods.

Lingua Franca

Amelia Fisher

I knew the children had no names, though I didn't understand it. Far had tried to explain it to me, but this was one barrier our strides in communication could not quite breach. She would always be of the city, and I an interloper. In the park, sitting on either side of the silent boy, you could have told that just from looking at us: Far in her machine-tailored suit jacket, me in my worn jeans and patchy self-applied buzz cut. Only one of us fully human, or so I'd been taught.

From the emotions flickering over their faces, I assumed she and the boy were engaged in silent conversation—or whatever the casters called it, since they insisted there were no words. I wasn't sure how letting the boy pick a name he'd never use was supposed to help with his tutoring lessons, but Far had insisted—said it would give the kid something to brag about to his friends. Personally, I doubted any of our pupils ever spoke a word outside of our sessions. Still, I figured there were things she wasn't telling me, or was unable to tell me as a result of what she would sardonically call my 'impairment'. But I'd learned when to stop asking questions long before I set foot in the city itself.

Far sat at the boy's side, leaning over his shoulder to scan the list of names with a kind, flavorless smile. The thermal regulators set at intervals along the grass softened the spring chill, warping the air around them with distortions of heat. The book propped up on the boy's grass-stained knees was made with real paper, a relic Far must have tracked down from some obscure online dealer. When I first came to the city, I probably would have taken offense at the laziness of that stereotype; it wasn't as if my sort hated technology. I said nothing. I'd been here long enough to know how these things went.

"Pine," Far said aloud. I'd gotten so used to the silence that the sound of a human voice was uncanny. "You like that name?" She met my eyes as she spoke. She always did, as if seeking out my approval, my appraisal of her accent, or maybe because really I was the one she was speaking to. The boy did not look up.

After that Far gave up on speaking in a way that I could perceive. I could hear the chirping of birds, the distant whisper of traffic drifting through the city's floating thoroughfares. Down the hill, children were tumbling over the playground like seed pods caught in a wind flurry, running pell-mell over the grass, hauling themselves up by their skinny arms and swinging back and forth on the hovering metal bars which always dipped lower before their strength gave out. Not one of them spoke, though at intervals they laughed at something I could not hear. They moved like images on a screen, detached from sound. From the dog park down the hill, a single low bark seemed to ride up to us on a vast wave of silence. Even the animals were quiet, well-trained. I kept quiet too.

"Well, that settles it," Far said at last. "Do you want to tell Vaun your name?"

At long last the boy looked up and met my eyes. "Kite," he said. His accent was much stronger than Far's, and the word sounded garbled on his unpracticed tongue. I'd learned to stop correcting him. That was Far's job. My job was to be a novelty and a prop.

"That's a nice name," I said. "What made you pick it?"

"The book had a picture."

"Like the bird, or the toy?"

The boy stared at me blankly for a long time before turning back to his teacher. In my pocket, my handheld buzzed an anxious tattoo of notifications. Probably the family group chat; the thought, sudden and cold, that it might be Nan gave me pause. Maybe my strange companions wouldn't mind if I pulled out my handheld in the middle of a session. They lived in a sea of notifications, after all; other people's thoughts and intentions were the air they breathed. Still, I had some sense of professional decorum. I ignored it for the time being.

Far waited patiently for a moment before saying; "Aloud, please. It's important to practice."

The boy—Kite, now, I supposed—did not sigh, but the conversation expected it. "How can one word mean more than one thing?"

Always so strange, to hear them vocalize. The words were correct enough, but something was missing in the speech itself, a lack of understanding or practice. She watched the boy, her expression unchanged. I noted her professionalism even if I didn't admire it. "It's rude not to include someone in the conversation."

"Not my fault she can't hear us." The more petulant he grew, the more natural his speech sounded. He looked at me then, full of that total stillness I could never convince myself wasn't hiding something else beneath. I met his gaze, trying not to make it a challenge, failing. Casters had no taboos against extended eye contact, and so we inspected each other for much longer than I could be comfortable with. I found myself studying his left eye for a glint of the thing behind it.

When he spoke at last, his expression did not change. "I'm sorry I was rude. I want to keep learning how to speak."

I wondered whether Far was feeding him the right words to say. Even that might be more effort than I should expect from her. "That's okay. Learning a language can be frustrating."

The boy's emotions moved over his face like storm clouds: doubt, irritation, boredom. But he still nodded—stiff, formal —and said, "Especially now that there's only one."

I blinked. "Well, there are quite a few spoken languages. We're speaking English right now, but many people speak Spanish, Chinese—"

His face did not change, but I heard Far sigh again. "No, you will only need to learn a single language to satisfy your extra-curricular requirement. Now, let's move on to the vocal warmups."

After the boy had been sent on his way, picked up by a sleek black car that lifted away from the park and into the transit loop above, Far and I settled at one of the park's many benches. She did this with the metal barrel of a cig between her lips, unlit as of yet, but placed there as soon as there was no chance of the boy or his chaperone seeing it. Her lips curled more easily around it than they did around her professional smile.

"Those aren't real names, you know. They're just words," I said, hating this urge to fill the silence and yet unable to resist it.

"Your 'real' names are just words."

"Old words."

"Oh, well that's alright, then." Far took a drag from her cig. "Let the kid have something to tell his parents."

Skirting the edge of a familiar argument, I decided to retreat. "How'd you pick your name?"

"Opened the dictionary and put my finger down at random." I doubted that. She'd probably done it a few times, until she found one she liked. *The state of being distant.* Words and sound still meant something, no matter what the casters liked to pretend.

In the lull of conversation, I slid my handheld from my pocket. Tocsin's name blinked up at me, but I caught Far staring at me and quickly put it away. She had whisked aside the benevolent placidity of her teaching facade as soon as the cig touched her lips. Now she just looked tired. The park was utterly silent but for the faint hum of the thermal regulators and the distant rumble of cars, the running footsteps of the voiceless children.

The tip of Far's cig flared green as she contemplated me. She might have spoken my language, but the way she looked at me was common to every caster I'd met— all overt, unfiltered feeling. No point keeping emotion off your face when everyone around you could skim it off the top of your biodigital cloud. A world without privacy, and thus without shame. Though sometimes Far's expressions were tinted by a more subtle quirk of her lips or eyebrow, or a sly look I couldn't quite read: expressions of a hidden interiority I liked to think she'd picked up from me. I sometimes wondered if she sent thoughts my way on impulse, a sleet of hellos and goodbyes and questions and jokes that slid off me without my knowledge.

It was that kind of thinking that made me doubt my choice sometimes, the thought of all those words and feelings falling mutely around me in a void I couldn't even feel. But then I'd remember what Nan always said: that the soul wasn't meant to be passed around like a cup of moonshine. How could there be trust without secrets?

Her arm over the back of the park bench shifted to where it didn't quite touch my back, but might have if I leaned back just a little. Again my handheld buzzed against my leg, but if I took it out now, Far would assume I was brushing her off. And, well, I had my own expectations about how this afternoon was going to end.

"How long before you have to go back?"

Before answering, I leaned over to pluck the cig from her lips and raise it to my own, breathing in the taste of—

"*Soap?*" I said, making a face as I handed it back.

Far grinned. "Cilantro. New flavor."

"I can see why no one thought of it before." But then I leaned back against the softness of her coat sleeve resting on the back of the bench and said, "Long enough."

After we were done, I peeled my cheek from the rise and fall of Far's rib cage with a sound like pulling off a piece of tape. The temperature modulator hummed busily from the ceiling, dumping a waterfall of chilly air into the otherwise stuffy room, turning my bare skin clammy. Far said nothing as I unspooled myself towards the other side of the bed where the glass of water always sat. Far watched me; I didn't need augmented mental senses to feel her eyes on the curve of my spine.

It had started with an argument about Borges, one of his collections Far was 'muchly surprised' I hadn't read. I'd taken issue with her tone and openly doubted that she owned a copy. By the time we got back to her place, I'd forgotten it entirely. I probably shouldn't have let things continue, but I was never very smart about that sort of thing. Far was available, attractive, and not from the compound, which made things both simpler and more complicated in a way that excited me. And it was a little cute, the way Far spoke; the ornate synonyms and slurring pronunciation, the accent of one who still tasted the words like they were new.

When I looked back, she had tucked one arm behind the back of her head, displaying a dark tuft of hair trimmed to a fashionable length. I couldn't imagine Far doing anything that wasn't fashionable. Her eyes were soft as a piece of fruit that you wouldn't want to eat. She opened her mouth and I braced myself for some brutal insight brought on by the candor of the afterglow.

But what she actually said was, "Can I have some of that water?"

I tipped my head back and drained the glass while holding her eye.

Far sighed. "You're a dick. Is that the right word here? Or would asshole be more appropriate?"

I got up to refill the glass from the nodule on the wall, cool water chilling the glass cupped in my fingers. When I brought it back to her and settled it on the soft dampness of Far's stomach, she sucked in a sharp, relishing breath.

"Neither," I said. "I'm very considerate."

"Hm. You have your moments."

The bob of her throat as she swallowed seemed to move inside of me, too. But what sank into the pit of my stomach wasn't an echo of the unspoken vows we'd been mouthing into each other's bodies for the past hour and a half. Only then I remembered my handheld's frequent buzzing. I fumbled it off the bedside table and was greeted with a storm of notifications. I swiped through them quickly, sliding them across the cool glass like oil over water, and all of them from Tocsin.

Home soon?

Hey dickhead I need to talk to you about smthn

turn your handle on or I'll tell Nan about your porn

For real, where are you?

Vaun, I'm serious.

Let me know when youll be back…

Vauneant?

it's important

hello???

And then, two hours later: *everything's fine but please come talk to me when you can and please don't ask anyone else about me.*

"Shit," I said aloud.

Far shifted against the covers. "Something wrong?"

Thirty-two messages total. If something truly dire had gone down, I'd have heard from more people—I'd have heard from Nan. Tocsin was more brother than cousin to me, but he was also an impulsive little shit, and always dealing with one self-manufactured personal crisis or another. It was probably about a girl, or a wrecked car. Probably nothing at all.

"Not sure," I said, sitting back down on the bed. "I should probably go."

Far turned to look at me. The way she used her eyes sometimes, it made me understand what casting was. "You know, maybe you wouldn't have to run around so much if you were making enough money to actually live on."

"You have some new clients for me?"

"I'm not talking about the tutoring. I'm talking about an actual job. If you were willing to use a temporary implant, they'd have no objection—"

"Not an option."

"Why not?" Anger sparked in Far's eyes; any attempt to hide it would have been alien to her. "I'm not going to argue with you about your aversion to implantation tech, I know that's no use." Knew that from long experience. "But a temporary one, Vaun? What's wrong with that? You wouldn't even have to tell anyone else—"

"And when I conveniently started making the kind of money that only comes from working at a caster place?" Most businesses these days would reject you out of hand as soon as they found out you didn't have an implant. A slurry of words: company culture, transparency, workflow. Who wouldn't want to hire an employee you never had to give a drug test, and whose productivity you could track just by sitting in the same room?

"Shit. This isn't how I wanted to tell you." She rolled over to the other side of the bed, waved the drawer of the nightstand open and dipped her hand into its darkness to withdraw a small glass vial with a dead worm inside. No, not dead; as she moved it towards me it gave a feeble twitch in its sterilizing liquid. Even from here I could see the way the mouth of the tube was shaped to fit perfectly against the socket of an eye, forming a perfect seal for the gel to settle against lid and lash before the digital tunneler did its work.

"It's a biodegradable model," Far said. In her voice, she had already won. "About a three-month half-life. They're actually *more* expensive than the permanent ones, you know. And if you'd just apply for a job that would cover—look. That doesn't matter. With this, I could have something lined up for you in a matter of days. Something that would actually pay. And I could help you. Tell you what to expect, coach you through the effects." She shifted closer. It struck me in a distant way that this little scene was exactly what Nan had probably envisioned when I told her I got a job in the city. She'd always said that corruption would be seductive.

I pulled away.

Before Far could reach for me, I was out of the bed, shoving various limbs into various articles of clothing, hoping I matched up the right holes.

"Vaun. Wait. *Wait.*" Far stumbled out of bed after me, flailing for a robe at its foot that she only managed to get half on. I couldn't tug my boots on before her hand settled on my shoulder. "Listen. I wasn't trying to offend you—"

"You have no idea what you're asking me to risk."

"God damnit, Vaun, that's because you never tell me!"

"There are plenty of things about me that you wouldn't understand."

"If you had the implant, I wouldn't have to—" She cut herself off before I could do it for her. Far's face was flushed. She didn't fight the tide of her anger. There was something comforting in knowing that for all the teeming life that existed beneath the surface of her, at least that surface couldn't lie.

"Alright," she said, and just like that the anger began to fade. "Alright. Just— this is an option, alright? I got it for *you.*

And it'll be waiting, whether you change your mind or not."

I watched her cross the room and put the thing back into the drawer. When she turned to me, she didn't bother to pull her robe shut, and I didn't bother not to look.

"Stay a little longer?" she said. There were times when she really could speak like a natural. But even as she stepped forward and leaned in, my eyes stayed open, on that bedside drawer. Visions of her holding it over my eye socket as I slept played with the gruesome relish of a slasher film. When she pulled back, I couldn't shift my eyes back fast enough.

"Gotta get back," I said, and her mouth did that thing that was almost a smile. Casters never were good at faking expressions.

"I just want to help," she said, and that was the worst part.

I leaned in to kiss her again, closed-lipped right up until the end, because I knew I'd want to be back here and wouldn't want to spend the next time putting out the fires I left burning today. Her fingers curled in the fleece-lined collar of my jacket, the grip light and brittle as the dry curl of the thing in the vial. I let it linger before pulling away. I was pretty good at tolerating things by now.

I scrolled through Tocsin's messages as the train slid free of the glass sheath at the edge of the city and began to pick up speed. *On my way back. You good?* I waited five minutes, refreshing my handheld, before slipping its cool weight back into my pocket. I almost pinged Tocsin's sister Coxcomb, but I knew better than to start asking around before I knew what Tocsin had gotten himself into.

The compound was only the last stop on the rail line in the loosest sense of the term. In reality you had to get off at the industrial district and walk another two miles down a road that was more weed than asphalt, cross-hatched with tar that could never hold the bursting cracks closed for long. Eventually you got to a chain link gate with a keypad—not exactly friendly, but we'd had our share of teenage casters prowling the perimeter, always in packs, silent, sometimes lobbing a rock or can of beer over the fence. No one else came out here, no one kept track of us, no one cared what was done to us or what we did to each other. I punched buttons so worn any idiot could probably guess the code, and stepped inside.

I could hear it before I saw it, the threads of noise breaking through the quiet like lightning in a summer storm. High raucous laughter, shouts of greeting or admonition, the clatter of doors and feet and conversations. I made my way down the central road through town, raising my hand to a few passing groundcars which honked at me as they crunched over the gravel. This time of day, most people were sitting out on their porches to watch the street, tinny songs blaring on their radios, the ice in their glasses clinking. More than a few had patches over their eyes.

The commotion on the Lin family's porch stopped me short before I reached my place. The usual crowd was gathered there, but today it didn't seem friendly. People lingered on the lawn to watch and listen and comment to their friends—arguments were a spectator sport. I couldn't make out the words, but I didn't really have to. I just had a hard time believing anyone in that household would have gone and put that thing in their head, knowing the consequences. I kept walking, grateful no one saw me and called me over to join them. I had to be careful about sharing my opinion on this kind of thing. People tended to assume I was biased, seeing as I worked in the city and was probably halfway to contaminated as a result. Nan certainly seemed to think so.

The lights were on in my house as I made my way up the path, and I could hear the sound of clanging pots and voices inside, the familiar hiss of the old oven. Grandpa Heimal was in his chair on the porch, as he always was unless someone forgot to wheel him out. The socket of his left eye clung to the shadows like a cave. He'd been one of the early-adopters, and he'd paid for it. By the time talk of malfunctions started slipping past the NDAs and corporate cover-ups, the implant had scrambled Heimal's brain from the inside out.

Nan did what she could for him, and for the others she found who'd been through the same. I sometimes wondered whether she left his hollowed-out eye socket uncovered as a reminder to all the rest of us. That was certainly Nan's style. I squeezed his shoulder as I walked to the door, and murmured a quick *hullo,*

Grandpa the way a Buddhist might turn the prayer wheels in passing.

From the moment I stepped inside, I was surrounded by warmth and light and familiar voices, so loud I could scarcely hear myself think as I took off my coat and my hat.

"Vauneant's back!" someone in the kitchen cried, and seconds later I was pelted at knee-height by a bundle of niece, grinning up at me from her grip around my knees.

"We're making lasagana!" Cispontine squealed.

I bent down to scoop her up, forcing an easy smile. "That's my favorite!"

"Vaun," my sister's voice called from the kitchen, "Get in here and make sure the vegetables don't burn."

Dutifully I trooped toward her voice, Cispontine on my hip. I could only glance at the stairs that led to the bedrooms before stepping into the kitchen. It was already packed in there, my cousin Snowbrowth fanning the smoke away from the detector, Cispontine's older sister sitting on the counter picking at the chips and dip, while uncle Groak tried to harangue her into helping peel vegetables.

"Did you hear about the Lins?" someone said in my ear, but no, I hadn't heard, and it was too loud to have it explained to me. Everyone was talking at once and I could hardly make out a word of it, and didn't need to try.

A couple times I checked my handheld. Still no response. I couldn't help but glance at the ceiling, the only thing which separated me from Tocsin's room. It seemed to sag toward me with the weight of whatever had happened. But I couldn't get away now without questions, and those could be dangerous around here.

At last, lasagna came out of the oven and the vegetables were oversalted, and Coxcomb finished doling out a healthy portion onto a plate and arranged it neatly on a tray.

"Take this up?" she said, as she always did, and for once I was glad to do it.

The stairs sighed under my boots as I made my way up. Nan's room made up the entire third floor, perched up top of the rest of the house like a watchtower. From up here you could see the entire compound, the endless green sprawl of forest and the glitter of the city on the horizon. Nan looked up from her work as I came in, her cane hooked on the edge of her workbench and small wire-frame glasses perched on her nose like something from an old digital film. She was the only person I knew alive who still used glasses; surgical eye correction was one modern amenity that the rest of us had all conceded to, but Nan said it was a manipulation of natural flesh, too close to changing who she was. Her glasses should have made her look sweet, old-fashioned; instead they focused her hard gaze into something that could have set the dried pages of Far's book alight.

I didn't look at the curtain in the back of the room, pulled closed against the makeshift surgery, and I didn't breathe through my nose. Still, the hint of chemicals prickled at my nose, imagined or not. This was the room where they did it—behind the curtain, the cot with disposable sheets and the blinking medical equipment, scrounged from outdated tech. Everything Nan might need to pull a long, biotech strand from a wayward eye socket. There was always a choice, of course, for anyone caught with an implant: take the operation or never come back.

"Nan," I said.

"Vauneant." She straightened, laying her soldering iron back in its cradle. I couldn't make sense of the wires and old-fashioned circuit boards in front of her. A piece of the temperature regulator, maybe. Nan was good at taking things apart and putting them back together to her own specifications. She'd been a doctor, before the compound; that fact had been one of the first to impress itself on my young mind. The use of old-fashioned computers, she'd taught herself out of necessity.

"Back from the city?" she said, with polite disapproval.

I stepped forward to put the tray on the table beside her. Her hair was the color of surgical steel where it caught the white light of her desk lamp. "Someone has to make sure those layabouts don't starve you."

Nan smiled, but her eyes still studied me the way they studied everyone. No one discussed the idea of moving her to a room downstairs. This had been her throne room as long as anyone could remember, and nothing short of death would unseat her from it.

Nan picked up the soldering iron again, and leaned over the pine-green circuit board. "Hear about the Lin boy?"

"Heard something happened. Not what."

A little line of smoke appeared from beneath the thin metal tool, curling up towards the hard shine of her glasses. She didn't specify, and I knew what that meant. What else of importance could happen to us here?

"It was just one of the temporaries, thank God," Nan said after a moment. "Just a matter of waiting for it to drain out of him. Still, the weakness revealed itself. His family will need to be diligent."

From what people told me of the time four decades ago, Nan had always been hard even when her face was soft. Maybe that was how she'd pulled this community around her like meat wrapped around bone, after she lost Heimal in all the ways that counted; and why our family out of all the rest was one of the few in the compound that hadn't turned up some wayward son or daughter who decided to put a biocomputer in their head. Ever since I'd gotten the job with Far, Nan had started looking at me like a sheep dog might look at a ewe with a limp.

"I'm sure they'll set him straight," I said, and Nan nodded, satisfied; she bent back over her workbench, and I knew I was dismissed.

Down the stairs once more, the air seemed easier to breathe. Tocsin's door was at the end of the hall, shut. I went to my room, loudly kicked off my boots, and made the rest of the way barefoot down the beaten-up runner. I knocked twice with one knuckle, soft as a branch tapping a window. There was no reply. I entered silently.

Tocsin lay in bed looking like he should be in the middle of an impact crater. He blinked up at me, barely able to raise his head as I closed the door softly behind me. He looked as young as he'd been when we rode down the stairs on our pillows, and as shell-shocked as when his head met the bottom bannister.

One of his eyes was bruised, the white of it gone painfully red.

"Hey, Vaun," he croaked.

I let out a slow breath as I settled next to him on the bed. For a minute we just sat there, turning over the silence between us like it was a puzzle that together we could somehow pick apart.

"Sure hope you didn't let anyone see you looking like that," I said after a while.

"I'm not an idiot, thanks."

"Would a smart person go and do what you just did?"

"I needed the work. *We* needed it," Tocsin said. Though we kept our voices low, I could hear the bitterness creeping in at the edges.

"At least tell me it's temporary."

"How the hell was I supposed to afford one of those?"

I put my head in my hands. "God damnit, Tocsin."

"What else could I do, huh? How long am I supposed to sit around all day watching Mom and Coxcomb live off canned protein and nutrient pills because none of us can get a job?"

"You think they'd be happier to know you went and did the one thing Nan would run you out of here for? You know the rules, Tocsin—"

"Yes, I know, *Jesus*, I know." Tocsin put a hand over his eyes, hiding the inflamed one from view. "I just need to make enough money to get by on for a while. Then I'll turn it off, and no one will ever need to know." He lowered his hands to look at me with an expression of wheedling accusation. "You know I would have found your kind of work if I could."

I turned away, hating to hear him say that. I was the example every parent in our compound told their kids about—Vaun who had found work in the city and still managed to stay unpolluted. My life was better in theory than in practice. Without the welfare checks and the fact that I wasn't paying rent, I'd never be able to keep my head above water.

"Listen," Tocsin said. He picked at the stray thread of his cuff instead of looking at me. "Nan is going to start to ask questions about the money this job is going to bring in. I was hoping you could —you know. Spread it around that I got work with your people. To help explain it."

I nodded, but because he wasn't looking, I had to force my dead tongue to move. "Of course. Don't even ask me that."

"Thanks." His voice was flat. Not ungrateful; just tired.

I cleared my throat. "You going to go to the support group?"

"It's called intunement, but yeah."

Indoctrination, as Nan would put it. Still, I was glad. We were in a distinct position out here to know how bad a mind could go once the implant cracked it open.

I made a vague gesture at his face. "How long will all that last?"

"Should fade by morning."

"Better hope it does," I said, knowing he knew I would cover for him if it hadn't. I thought of Nan's hard eyes drilling into my head, the curtain and the smell of disinfectant; and also of the warm currents of talk and food and companionship that made this place a home. I'd seen what had happened to other kids when their families found out they strayed; either an empty eye socket or an empty place at the table. In a way our world was defined by absence as much as Far's was by the lack thereof. Was it better to be mutilated in body, or soul?

For a while longer I sat there. Then I rose, unable to stay another minute in that close room with its prickling silence, wondering what Tocsin was hearing and feeling that I just couldn't reach. The truth was, I was scared for him. But I had no idea how to tell him that, and in the end it was easier to say nothing at all.

"It's not a cult."

Sitting at our customary bench, Far turned to me with a wry smile. "You're good with words, Vaun. But I'm not confident in your ability to reason that one out."

"I don't have to convince you that I'm *not* in a cult. The burden of proof is on you."

"Fine." Far passed me her cig, which glowed brown this time. I eyed it nervously, but inhaled all the same. The cinnamon tasted like vague relief. Kite's lessons had been going well for the past couple weeks, and the latest tutoring lesson had ended early. Far had yet to ask me back to hers today. I think maybe part of her enjoyed the illicit thrill of sitting in public and *talking*. That irritated me a bit, but the fact was I liked talking to her.

She hadn't brought up the vial waiting in her bedside drawer again, either. I'd checked, once, while she was in the bathroom—it was still there. It could afford to wait.

Far held up a finger. "You live on a compound. You distrust outsiders. You reject modern technology for religious reasons—"

"It's not religion," I said, a little too sharply. I didn't like the way she was ticking my life off on her fingers like plot points in a hack novel.

Far looked at me, calculating. "You can believe in something religiously without any sort of God coming into it."

I looked away, biting the inside of my cheek. "You forgot to mention the human sacrifice," I said, and Far laughed that ugly sawing laugh of hers that I'd reluctantly come to enjoy.

It wasn't as if I hadn't thought about it, I almost wanted to say. The doors that would open for me as soon as I let the world into my thoughts would change my life forever. But it would mean shutting another door behind me, the one which led to the only family and home I'd ever known. Birthed into the amniotic ocean of thought as she'd been, I didn't think Far could understand that.

"Come on," she said, slipping the cig back into her breast pocket. "It's a beautiful day. Let's walk to my place for once."

"You're assuming I want to come home with you."

"Yes, I am."

I rolled my eyes, a gesture that Far had never succeeded in duplicating. I ought to have told her I had somewhere to be, just to prove that I could still say no, but in the end the flesh was weak.

As we left the park, I was immediately glad to have Far at my side. Hanging trolleys whispered over our heads as they passed, sweeping over the shuffle of hundreds of feet and the soft hush of cars sliding past. The faces which passed were alight with a wash of silent emotion. The buildings were paneled with blank screens, grim and grey—only a caster could perceive what they were trying to sell.

There were others here, I knew, who had once been like me. Expats from the compound who'd kept their eyes and implants, and lost everything else. None had ever approached me. They'd been subsumed, just a few more silent ghosts wandering the city streets.

"Doesn't it bother you?" I asked. My words smeared that silence like an obscene stain. "The quiet."

Far snorted, tossing her long braid over her shoulder. She made more seemingly unconscious sound than any other caster

I had met. I wonder if the people around her thought her strange, or whether she could turn it on and off as easily as a switch in her head. "I could ask you the same question."

"And I'd tell you that it does. It bothers me a lot."

She shrugged. "It isn't quiet for me. I can cast into the thoughts of people around me, if I want to. Except yours."

"That sounds awful."

"Oh, I'm sure I'm not missing out on much." She sobered a little, turning to face me with her full interest. "The idea of walking around with cotton stuffed in my brain, numb and dumb to everyone—*that* sounds awful to me."

"Maybe I like keeping some things to myself."

"Interesting use of conditional, considering you're the most covert person I know. You'd tell me if you were some kind of murderer, right?"

"Depends. Can you keep a secret?"

Far laughed again, and then covered her mouth when a person passing us looked at her sharply. It was rude to break the quiet, and I felt a little good about that; like I'd managed to show her something about me, without even really trying. I supposed that to venture out of the city and into that vast silence where there was nothing to cast to or to cast back at you would be a kind of death to Far. A terrible thing, to be cut off from all you'd ever known.

Then she leaned over to peck my cheek, and I stopped thinking about unreachable worlds for a while.

"I really do want to know."

Far said this before I'd started getting dressed again, which was how I knew she might be serious. "Why is rejecting the implant so important to you and yours?" she continued, on seeing I was listening.

I propped myself up on a hand, thinking. She'd never asked before, not really, so I'd never had to explain it before. I thought about what Nan would say: that language made us human, and the implants made us something else. Having seen the city, it was hard to argue with that. But there was something more to it; something even Far might understand.

"Have you ever asked someone where they wanted to eat dinner, listened to them think aloud about what they're in the mood for, until you can both agree on something? Or do you just think *food* and pick up the general sensations and cravings of the person you're with?"

"I don't see the difference. We end up at the restaurant either way."

"There's no room for mistakes. For all the little things you lose and gain between thought to word to thought again."

Far raised her eyebrows. "Translations are imperfect by nature."

"Art is an imperfect translation."

"Now you're just being pretentious."

"Now I'm trying to make a *point*."

That familiar smile touched half her lips. "If only you had an implant. Imagine how easily you could convey your ideas."

It was a joke. It should have been easy to laugh it off. But I couldn't just then; I was thinking about Tocsin, and my grandfather's eye drifting like a dead log on a placid sea. When my gaze slid to Far again, her own face had gotten quiet.

"Vaun," she said. "If there were something bad happening out there, would you tell me?"

I pressed a kiss to the back of her hand in lieu of an answer, but in the end she took it as answer enough.

When I reached the final train stop within the city limits, the car emptied as if disemboweled. It was only me and an older woman who sat at the end, veined hands trembling over her handscreen. As soon as we passed a certain stop, a switch was triggered—now the spilling color over the walls had sound attached, music that poured out of the train's tinny speakers and startled me into alertness.

"With new implant technology, it's never been easier to upgrade," a cheerful baritone said as images flashed across the screen—people effortlessly finding each other across a crowded train station, a team of dancers coordinating in a complex routine, a mother casting at her baby for the first time. *"The world is waiting. Cast out for it."*

The ads were clearly targeted. In the end, no one would even have to force us— it would just happen slowly, as people gave in, realized it was easier to assimilate, told themselves they'd stay vocal with their families, their kids; but how many generations would it take for even that faint conviction to flicker out?

Glancing at the old woman at the other end of the train, I realized she was staring at me hard—and that she was probably trying to cast at me. When the train reached its final stop I got off quickly, leaving her behind.

The walk back to the compound went quickly, lost in my thoughts as I was. The sound of raised voices from beyond the chain link fence didn't strike me as particularly alarming until the gate rolled back on its aging motor and I saw the crowd.

They were gathered outside of my house.

I didn't realize I was running until the scene wavered and dragged me closer like something from a bad dream. No elbowing through the crowd tonight; people saw me and they split apart. Even from the outskirts I could see Nan on the porch, leaning on her walking stick. She only ever came down the stairs in a crisis. Now that crisis was seething around my home like antibodies around a virus.

And then Nan's eyes shifted to me, and nothing in her expression or posture changed; it was just that I bore the full weight of her attention like the muzzle of a gun held inches from my forehead. People were asking her questions, asking *me* questions, but all I could do was stand there skewered by her gaze. I knew she knew I'd kept Tocsin's secrets, and that made me hardly any better than him.

I cleared the porch steps in two strides, my eyes shifting from Nan to the door. I just had to get to Tocsin. But before I could step forward, a hand shot out to catch my arm in a grip you'd only use on an animal, something whose pain didn't need respecting. Behind her glasses, Nan's eyes bored into mine.

"It's done," she said. I tried to tear away, but she held me fast. "We gave him the choice," Nan said, each word another chunk bitten out of me. "He chose *us*."

I was not deaf to the inference, the silent second half of her sentence: the choice that I had made, without ever knowing I had made it. I stared into Nan's eyes, but they were flat behind the glass. I thought of Coxcomb and Cispontine and Groak, the noise and love and connection. No one stepped forward to speak for me now. The silence around me bled like a wound.

Nan let me go. I stumbled, nearly fell into someone; I didn't see or care who. The door, the house—someone tried to stop me, but I heard Nan's voice. "Let her say her goodbyes. She'll be gone within the hour."

I turned on her. Numbness spread through my chest like a branching tree of dead nerves. "I should get a choice," I said, my voice hollow. "You give everyone a choice."

Nan shook her head. "You already made it."

I turned around. The house was empty as a tomb. Up the stairs. My eyes stung and swam, but I kept moving. Tocsin's door was open, vacant. It was Nan's room I went to; the door was unlocked, the computer parts on the workbench all filed into the separate compartments of her plastic storage container. The curtain on the other side of the room had been drawn back. I saw the bright red biohazard bin first, the color snagging my eye. The blink of the machines: pulse, breath, things that made no sense to me. Half of Tocsin's face had a piece of medical gauze taped over it, and where once the eye had lain beneath it there was a rose of blood budding in the cotton, unfurling with each beep of the machines. Still sedated. We weren't barbarians, tearing out the eyes of our unwilling victims without proper medical procedure. That was the worst of it, of course—that in the end, Tocsin had chosen this. As much as you could choose anything, when the alternative was to be stripped of everything you'd ever known and loved.

I sat by his bedside a long time, knowing he wouldn't wake for hours. Even if he had, I knew what he'd probably say.

No one tried to stop me as I left. They went silent as I passed. I spread it around me like a stench. The sun was going down, and there were no lights on the long cracked road back to the train station. In the dark, all I could see was the spot of blood. I knew I'd never walk this road again. What was wrong with me wasn't something they could pluck out.

I sat on the steps to Far's building for a long time, waiting for her to see my message. I'd only sent the one; I couldn't dig up the words, the urgency, the hour, the year. I didn't know how I'd found my way here, other than following something I hadn't known was inside of me. The city was utterly silent but for the occasional sound of footsteps. It didn't bother me now. I never wanted to hear a spoken word again.

When the door behind me opened I jerked like someone caught nodding off. And then Far was in front of me, her arms gripping her elbows. Her eyes were confused, and a little scared, and darted between me and the heavy backpack leaning against my leg.

"Um." I followed her gaze to my pack. For a moment I lost myself in its shape and contours, which seemed more real to me than anything else had ever been in my life. It occurred to me in a distant way that this might be asking too much; that Far might actually turn me away. "I know you don't have any reason to—"

"Get in here," she said with hoarse exasperation, as if there had never been any other answer at all. She led me to her door, or she must have—I didn't feel awake or alive in the strictest sense of the word. Eventually I was naked, in her bed, and she was molded to me, chaste and still clothed. For once, I wanted to tell her everything. I wanted to open my mouth and let it pour out of me like bile dredged up from deeper than retching should go. My tongue was stone. I smelled disinfectant on every breath.

I reached for the gleam before my eyes, the single point of light: the metal knob of the bedside table that I had opened a hundred times in my mind. Far's hand tangled with mine before I could fumble inside. She pulled my hand back and pressed it to my chest until I could feel every beat of my heart as clearly as if I held it in the palm of my hand.

"Shh," she said, and stroked my hair. "Shh."

And for a while there was silence deeper than I had ever known, and in Far's arms I drank from it until I was full.

See Amelia Fisher's story "Lingua Franca"
online at Metaphorosis.
If you liked it, leave a comment. Authors love
that!
Remember to subscribe to our e-mail updates so
you'll know when new stories are posted.

About the story

The first version of "Lingua Franca" bears little resemblance to the way it ended up. The concept I began with was, why does telepathy always involve language? If people could communicate mind-to-mind virtually from birth, directly sharing images and emotions and ideas, what use would there be for words? What does a society with communication but no language look like?

Having conceived of a society which communicated exclusively through mind-impressions, I figured I'd better introduce a non-telepathic character to explore it on the reader's behalf. Thus the idea of the spoken word tutoring sessions arose, and a character balanced halfway between two worlds, trying to bridge them both.

The initial draft involved a sort of seduction in the opposite direction: Vaun wanted to introduce Far to the miracle that is human language, with all its quirks and miscommunications. Over the course of writing the story, I ended up reversing that. Since this telepathy was technological in origin, I figured there would be intense pressure on anyone who decided not to take the implant. Overall, "Lingua Franca" began as an exploration of language, and privacy, and two people from very different worlds attempting to form some kind of connection.

And then I hit the point that I always run into with my stories, where I go "but what if it was a horror story?" And thus, the more cultish elements emerged. I ultimately eased back from true horror, and settled on something that felt more authentic: the claustrophobia and joy that go hand-in-hand with any tight-knit community.

I realized at a certain point that my ruminations on language and privacy were really prodding at what it means to be human at all—is being an individual a requirement? Is shame? At the end of the day I feel like I picked up and turned over a lot of questions I can't really answer, but I certainly enjoyed the asking.

A question for the author

Q: Do you generally start with mood, title, character, concept...?

A: I'm an ideas-gal. I love to start with a big, weird, capital-C Concept. When I stumble across a world or scenario full of questions and potential, I start looking for the tension point: the moment or location or character that makes the story come alive. Once I have a general idea of what kind of world or situation I want to explore, the first line usually staggers in, fashionably late and slightly inebriated, and the story takes off from there.

About the author

Amelia Fisher writes queer speculative fiction from her home in Vancouver, Washington. She likes plants, tea, and Cordyceps fungus.

ameliafisher.com, @hubristicfool

Holding

John Adams

I never cared much about cars as a kid—never cared much about anything Dad liked. The older I got, the more he and I argued. About school. Guys I dated. Hell, who ate the last piece of birthday cake.

My last clear memory of him is my 15th birthday. I'd let a pudgy gray cat follow me home—Nottingham, I think I called it. "I told you no pets, Kerry," Dad yelled. "Your mom's allergic, and I'm not paying the extra deposit!" He scooped up the cat and stormed out of the apartment.

Dad died a few weeks later.

I never saw that cat again.

It's late, and I'm still at Dorsey's Auto Repair, my place of employment. Dad's place of employment. After he died, I got more interested in cars. I signed up for Shop class in 12th grade. Enrolled in vo-tech after high school. Cornered Dorsey the day after graduation, announcing I was ready to work. Dorsey was so flustered, he didn't have the gall to say 'no'.

Tonight, I'm on the creeper platform, wheeled under Mrs. Moritz's 2008 Nissan Sentra: 3,000-ish pounds of steel, aluminum, and hand-knitted afghans. Sweet lady. Bad driver. This is the second time we've had to replace her catalytic converter because of 'that ornery curb on Maple Street' that always seems to jump in front of her car on her way back from the craft store.

I slink my arm behind me and grab another spring bolt. I slab some lube on it and work it into the converter. Two bolts left after this one, and then I can go home.

Something rattles from the storeroom. I jerk in the tight space, almost banging into Mrs. Moritz's undercarriage. Mice. Dorsey warned me. I don't usually work this late, so I've never heard them before. "Nothing to be scared of," Dorsey said.

Funny. I've seen things that would scare Dorsey way more than mice.

I reach behind me and fumble for the two remaining bolts. I pinch one between my fingers, work it into one of the threaded slots, and tighten it with the torque wrench.

My friends ask if it's... weird. They always put that pause before 'weird.' Is it... weird to work where my dad died? Do I work here out of... (that pause again) family loyalty?

But it's not loyalty.

See, I'm a good mechanic. Could've worked anywhere. I picked Dorsey's not because of my loyalty. I picked Dorsey's because of my skills. And I don't mean my car skills.

When I was seven, Uncle Frank died. At his wake, everyone cried. Everyone except me. I played checkers in the basement. With Uncle Frank. Just like we used to. A shimmering, flickering version of Uncle Frank.

Uncle Frank was the first of many.

Some people stick around the places they die.

'Haunting' is too strong a word.

I call it 'holding.'

I call them 'holders.'

It doesn't happen all the time. I can go for months, once even more than a year, between holders. But sometimes... sometimes, I see them. Sometimes, I hear them, feel them. Sometimes, I even get flashes of their lives. Moments that were important to them, even if I don't always understand the context. Like that girl in the Muppet Babies T-shirt; when she walked closer to me, I flashed on her, many years ago, sitting in a dirty kitchen, eating licorice. The woman with the scar; she whispered in my ear, and I flashed on her, her face smooth and perfect, crying over a torn letter. The young minister; he fumbled to take my hands in his flickering grasp, and I flashed on his church, watching him clutch his chest and keel over.

I don't know if Dad's a holder. But since I was 15 years old, I've needed him to be. Needed to see him again. Needed to understand why he did what he did. It's why I started working at Dorsey's. The place where he worked. The place where he died. The place where he took his own life.

I reach back and run my hand along the cold concrete floor.

The final bolt is gone.

I swallow hard.

I know better than to hope. Know how unpredictable holdings and holders are. Know I probably just knocked the bolt aside.

I whisper it anyway: "Dad?"

I slowly roll the creeper out and stand. I wipe my greasy hands on my coveralls, more routine than formality. Dad won't care.

There's a rustling in the storeroom. And a faint clinking.

Maybe it's not mice after all.

I edge to the small room, peeking into the doorway. Inside, dead-center, batting around the bolt, is a cat. No. Not a cat. The cat. Nottingham. The tubby gray tabby I snuck into the apartment as a teenager.

The cat flickers, shimmers. It's a holder.

I laugh. This is a first. "What are you doing here, Naughty Boy?" I ask, immediately remembering the nickname.

Head cocked curiously, Nottingham meows at me before rearing back on gray haunches and leaping onto a metal shelf. I watch, amused, as the holder-cat jumps between two shelving units, higher and higher. Nottingham stops at a cardboard box near the top, tail twitching, and turns to me, releasing a pained mew.

"What's in there, Naughty Boy?"

I push over Dorsey's footstool, step up, and pull down the box. Nottingham is back on the ground before I am.

I strip off yellowed tape and open the dusty box. It's one of Dorsey's junk caches. The cat head-butts the box, and I start unpacking items. Metal scraps. Bolts. Lugs.

But that's not all I unpack. I see images, flashes—like the flashes I sometimes see from human holders, but softer, less focused. Dad petting Nottingham as he drives from our house. Dad making Nottingham a cozy bed in this very box. Dad hiding Nottingham under Dorsey's nose all those years ago.

When I get to the bottom of the box, there's something else. Seven somethings, in fact.

Because Nottingham isn't a naughty boy. She's a desperate mama.

Seven shimmering kittens, each of them holders, mew as Nottingham hops inside, nuzzling them. I see a flash of Nottingham giving birth one night, Dad watching over them, nervous but fascinated. He looks excited, like when he used to try to teach me about engines. But also... he's about to cry. I don't think I ever saw him cry when he was alive, but it's like I know that look on him. Like I know him. He holds something in his hands. The vision is fading, so I struggle, concentrate, and I just barely make it out. It's a photo. Him and me. That summer when I was eight and we went to Six Flags. He looks from the photo to the kittens and back to the photo again.

The flash dissolves.

I'm back in the present.

I know if I wanted, I could see more flashes—flashes of what happened to the cats, how they ended up as holders in Dorsey's storeroom.

But I don't want to. Don't need to. Just because something ended—even ended horribly—doesn't mean there wasn't still goodness, still happiness, still gray-fluffball sweetness before that.

Maybe that's enough.

I scurry to Mrs. Moritz's car, grab one of her afghans, and return to the box. The babies knead their tiny paws on Nottingham's belly. I whisper, "Good girl," and lay the afghan around them.

I don't know if they can feel it.

But I sure can.

See John Adams's story "Holding" online at Metaphorosis.
If you liked it, leave a comment. Authors love that!
Remember to subscribe to our e-mail updates so you'll know when new stories are posted.

About the story

I generally write speculative fiction that is humorous, gothic, or some combination of humorous and gothic; I tell people my wheelhouse is "Dark Shadows with space monkeys". On the flip side, when I write non-speculative fiction, I tend to go for more dramatic moments — high-school friendships put to the test, relationships ending, managing through loss, and those moments we'd rather read about on the page than experience in real life.

With "Holding", I wanted to merge these two ideas and write a dramatic piece of spec-fic. I have written several ghost stories before, but never one with quite this tone. To me, the piece has a sadness to it, but still remains hopeful.

The story centers on the idea that sometimes what we think we want isn't what we actually want. I have to quote the Rolling Stones here, because they said it best: "You can't always get what you want, but if you try sometime you find you get what you need". I think those lyrics sum up the story well.

I also wanted to provide an ending that felt satisfying even though it didn't necessarily solve every mystery — perhaps even satisfying -because — it didn't solve every mystery. The main character, Kerry, may not have all her questions answered by the end, but she ultimately finds comfort.

Thanks for reading, and thanks to Metaphorosis for giving me this great opportunity!

A question for the author

Q: What tools do you write with?

A: I'm fairly basic when it comes to writing tools — I arm myself with a laptop, a frequently broken wireless mouse, and a cat who chews on the laptop cord. I've purchased several fancy journals with the sincere intention of writing long-hand, but my hands cramp after a few minutes and I can barely read my own penmanship.

About the author

John Adams (he/him/his) is a short-story, stageplay, and screenplay writer. He enjoys creating robust, offbeat worlds populated with teenage detectives, pelican-people, robo-butlers, cursed cowboys, and bear nuns. When not writing, he produces comedy shows and performs across the U.S. with That's No Movie, a multi-genre improv-comedy team. He lives in the Kansas City area, where he works as a communications professional.

johnamusesnoone.com, @JohnAmusesNoOne

Tower of Mud and Straw

Yaroslav Barsukov

II. The Adversary

This is part 2 of Yaroslav Barsukov's novella, *Tower of Mud and Straw*. Part 1 ran in September 2020. What has gone before:

Minister Shea Ashcroft refuses the queen's order to gas a crowd of protesters. After riots cripple the capital, he's exiled to Owenbeg, a duchy bordering the kingdom of Duma, to oversee the construction of the biggest anti-airship tower in history. Shea doesn't want the task, but sees it as the only way to reclaim his life.

The duchy serves as a home to Drakiri, refugees of a technologically advanced human-like race.

Once in Owenbeg, Shea is shocked to learn the artisans are using the 'tulips'—anti-gravity devices created by Drakiri, devices from a place in Shea's memories he would rather erase. He considers the 'tulips' to be volatile and dangerous.

The duke of Owenbeg is none too happy about the arrival of an intendant from the capital and orders Patrick, his military counselor, to get rid of him. Shea is saved by the duke's lover, Lena, who turns out to be half-Drakiri; Lena tells him that her race had once built a huge tower similar to the one in Owenbeg, which allowed a *second edifice* to manifest. Drakiri call the second tower the 'Mimic Tower' and believe it to be a portal into a different, frightening dimension. Back then, they managed to destroy their tower and prevent the nightmare from creeping into the world. Shea discounts Lena's story as a children's tale.

Shea has no real allies and only the memory of his dead sister to converse with. The duke's people accidentally slip information that someone has tried to sabotage the construction site; however, after visiting the tower, Shea forms a theory that there were no saboteurs, only artisans meddling with the technology they couldn't begin to understand. After a clash with the duke he manages to get the 'tulips', the anti-gravity devices, removed from the tower.

He's then visited by Brielle, the tower's chief engineer, who reveals her secret: she's made an error in the calculations. The tower's foundation is too small to support its height, and the 'tulips' were the only thing holding the structure together. By insisting on having them removed, Shea has doomed the tower and lost any chance of getting back his life.

1

The hammer fell in an arrhythmic pulse, like an old man's heart, skipping a punch each time the chisel it hit dropped another inch into the device. And each time, the sheath's halves spread wider, the pink glow which seeped along the expanding crease thickened, and the man in the protective mask shrank back.

"It's dangerous, you do realize that," Shea said. "The thing could implode."

Brielle stared, without blinking, in front of her. "Now I understand why you call them 'tulips'. They blossom, don't they?"

They blossom all right, he thought. *They jump seasons while we remain here, in this autumn.*

The wind rose and combed through the crown of the old overgrown oak, hurling a handful of leaves at the Drakiri devices arranged in rows at its foot. *We, too, throw dirt on coffins—only ours don't have pointed ends.* The 'tulips' stood upright, taking aim at the sky. The man with the hammer and the chisel was human, but the two figures frozen beside him were Drakiri—Shea had learned to recognize them by now, the slightly elongated physique, the too-relaxed posture. *None of them would work at the construction site,* Lena had said—apparently, supervising the dismantling of the devices was a different thing.

A strange threesome—with many other such threesomes scattered across the field among the egg-shaped things.

"It's like attending a mass funeral," Shea said.

"Do you want to say a few words, then?"

"Bad time of the year to develop a sense of humor, Brielle. How much longer before *it* crumbles?" It, *and what remains of my life.*

The giant tower was an apparition now, pastel-gray and watery past the fields.

"What, you can't count days anymore?" she asked. "I haven't seen you in a while—

when did you last leave your new quarters?"

Shea shrugged. "A week, maybe. I don't know." He glanced at her. "Wait a second —you're judging me, aren't you? As if you weren't drinking yourself."

"I drink just enough to keep my sanity."

"Well, perhaps my sanity requires a higher dosage."

The tulip let out a loud crack, making a flight of black birds disperse from the oak's branches and the man with the hammer start back. The chisel remained lodged in the crease: a knife in a wound.

One of the Drakiri said something in a reassuring tone.

"Do you know what's inside?" Brielle asked.

"No. Ten years ago, we had no method for disassembling them."

"What did you do?"

"Buried them." His thoughts darted to the room with soot stains, but this time didn't stay there: he remembered the cellar underneath the rosewood trapdoor, the memory answering in dull tones as though someone had picked at a scab. He shook his head. "I don't understand why they can't have the Drakiri do the procedure."

"That's the crux of the joke: we have a lighter touch. I heard one of *them* say—"

"We were born to destroy these things."

"—we were born to disassemble them."

The sheath fell apart in eggshell pieces.

Inside, the tulip was almost empty. A thin stem stretched the whole height of the device, swelling with purple that squirmed like air in a heatwave, widening in the middle to form a...

"It's a figure, isn't it?" Shea said, or thought he had.

The contour of a leg, a hint at a hip, maybe an armless torso. Or maybe it was his imagination going wild. The Drakiri who'd spoken earlier produced something resembling a pair of pliers which he fastened, simultaneously, to both ends of the 'silhouette.' He held the pliers while the purple and the quivering died down, then, the stem at arm's length, wandered off to the tree line, to a funeral pile of other thin, long things.

The man in the mask picked up the chisel and moved toward the next tulip.

"And that's how the mundane trumps the beautiful," Shea said. "Let's go. Nothing more to see here."

He turned when he heard a quiet, "I'll fix the tower."

"What? You said the foundation was too small."

"It is. But I did some calculations yesterday—maybe, if we fortify the walls…"

"You don't believe it yourself."

"I'll try fortifying the walls."

"Brielle, listen to me."

"What do you want me to do, Shea?" She leaned toward him, and, through clenched teeth, her breath came out in a miniature cloud. "Sit back and see it crumble? Not even attempt to save the work of my life?"

He took her by the arm. "Think of the builders' safety."

"They're safe, trust me. The strain on structure won't start taking its toll for two months."

"Okay. Okay. Listen, Brielle, I give you —us—two months. Then we turn ourselves in to Queen Daelyn."

He immediately regretted not having phrased it differently—Brielle's anger dissipated the way air leaves a balloon, and, as with the tulip, what remained behind was a vulnerable stem.

"Please don't tell anyone until then, Shea. Please. Don't tell them... of the mistake I've made."

It's not your fault, he wanted to say, *it was probably the time pressure, and nobody is infallible*—but at that moment, Brielle chuckled.

"Look, the asshole's coming."

Through the rows of devices, a tall, hunched figure moved like a tired priest, fed up with performing the final rites.

"Did you know the duke has put him in charge of the disassembling? It's like a penance for all that talk that amounted to nothing, about the saboteurs."

Patrick, the duke's military counselor, strolled toward them, beating the wet out of the flaps of his coat. He stopped in front of Brielle and glanced at her.

"Destroying the devices is a waste of time." He smiled only with his lips. "A pure waste of time and money. Whatever *he* says, the damage to the tower was a result of sabotage."

"Hey, I'm right here," Shea said.

Patrick shifted his gaze to him, and his mouth opened and closed as though the body were looking for the best way to pour out contempt.

"There's a special type of capital swine," he said, "that comes to our lands and shits on them."

"How did Shea shit on *your* land, Patrick?" Brielle sighed. "You're not even originally from Owenbeg."

"And you, you should know better, Brielle. Are you sleeping with him?"

"That's enough," Shea said. "Just because we're standing here and talking, man and woman, you automatically presume that we share a bed?"

But Patrick didn't accept the challenge; he simply shrugged, straightened his coat, walked past them.

Shea turned to look at him. "He sounds depressed more than anything. The duke's displeased with him, right?"

Brielle nodded. "Some important task that Patrick has failed."

The one where he had to dispose of me, probably.

"Besides," she said, "he's been promising to catch the Dumian saboteurs for months."

"There are no saboteurs."

Against the swollen gray sky, Patrick's figure stuck out like a finger, and, with surprise, Shea realized he couldn't bring himself to hate him.

Brielle sighed. "I still have my doubts—and, as you can see, Patrick does, too."

How could he hate the bastard? *Daelyn's power eroded me, the duke's—him. Patrick simply had less substance to begin with.*

"I'm going," Shea said. "If you wish, let's meet at the tavern and discuss our situation."

"Tomorrow?"

"No. The day after. I will be incapacitated tomorrow."

In the new quarters he would no doubt have to vacate soon, Shea opened the wine cabinet and looked at the empty bottles. Tuesday, they were called, Wednesday, Thursday, Friday, Saturday. Tuesday had been his first in years—he'd bought it himself, same as Wednesday; the rest had come in linen sacks a boy from the village carried.

With the Drakiri devices destroyed, the tower's collapse became imminent, and it was time to send for stronger stuff.

2

She appeared at his doorstep clad in a gray hunting suit, and although the brandy's kerosene aftertaste still corroded his mouth, he smiled.

Will you join me?

Sure, sure I will. It was okay. The room wasn't spinning, so the alcohol the boy Daniel had brought must've been thinned with water.

It was only three miles later, halfway between the castle and the forested hillside, that Shea realized how wrong he'd been.

"Are you okay?" Lena's voice came from somewhere to his right.

"Yes. I think so."

His own words echoed as though emerging from the bottom of a huge metal bowl; the world around him, streaming past, adjusting itself to fit the curves and turns of the trail they followed.

"I thought you could use a distraction —Brielle said you haven't left your quarters for a week." Her voice wrapped around him like a scarf snatched and tossed by the wind. "We need to pick up speed. The deer is getting away."

A wave of dizziness washed over Shea. *I think I'm about to fall.* He would fall, Brielle would fall, the tower would fall, his career would give its final death jerk.

The trees ahead parted—from between them, as if responding to his thoughts, the giant tower stared at him, bluish in the haze.

I hate you, he thought, *I hate you*, all the thousand feet of stone and metal, the artillery portals and the embers of the little worlds scattered across the spiral climb, *how I hate it all now*.

Lena stood in the stirrups. "There it is!"

Their prey darted into a clearing fifty feet ahead, a gray curve under a crown of bones.

For a moment, there were only the deer, the tower, and the beautiful woman, clinging to the horse's neck, shouting something into the wind.

Then the deer vanished.

That's it, they must've mixed something into that brandy.

The deer had disappeared like an object tumbling into the eye's blind spot, never to emerge on the other side.

He realized he wasn't imagining things when Lena's horse went mad. It slipped into a wild, erratic dance, the bucks and rears of a rocking toy, shaking its head in a motion that made it appear as if it were wagging its own body.

Lena pulled on the reins.

She needs to dismount. Did he say it out loud? *Lena, Lena, you need to...*

"Get off the horse!"

Of course she didn't listen. She leaned back, pushing against the stirrups, stretching the reins, her horse's mane a dark reflection of the wave of her own hair.

Shea kicked his mare into a gallop.

"Dismount!"

Still, she didn't listen. And when he got close enough to grab her by the arm, shook him off.

"Get off of it!"

Drakiri strength doubly worked against her now: it allowed her to brush Shea off and stressed her horse even further—a product of generations of breeding, it must've preferred a lighter, human touch.

Shea's belly spasmed, and he almost puked.

I need to do something, and fast.

Lena was at least twice as strong as him, true—but he weighed more.

He rammed his shoulder into hers, sending them both to the half-frozen autumn ground.

"Why did you do that?" She pushed him away, and he rolled off her and into the grass. "I would've gotten him under control. I would've calmed him."

"Shhh," he said, pointing to the horse, who dove under an elm's branches and disappeared behind the trees.

"What?"

"I haven't seen a purebred that spooked."

His own mare grazed peacefully nearby.

"Never do that to me." Lena slapped his arm. "Are you drunk?"

"It could've thrown you off and trampled on you. Or your foot could've slid through the stirrup, and it would've dragged you into the woods like a sack."

After a series of long breaths, she said, "Where did the deer go? Did it run back into the trail?"

It vanished, he wanted to say—but now, with the brandy loosening its grip on him, he was no longer sure. He closed his eyes and tried to recall the scene, but the kerosene taste in his mouth kept getting in the way.

"I'm not certain, Lena."

"You were behind me. If it returned to the trail, it should've passed you."

He shook his head.

"So you *are* drunk—how much did you have? Wait, don't tell me. I can't believe I went hunting with you." Staring at the sky, she drew in her knees, suddenly vulnerable. "I saw something. In a flash. Different colors."

"What, rainbows?"

"No. Forget it. I think it was a hallucination—or something like that. I got distracted, and that's when the deer ran away."

Lena rolled onto her side and started to get up, only to fall back, this time on top of Shea.

"Damn it." She laughed. "My hip hurts like hell, I must've pulled a muscle."

"You're the only woman I know," he said, "who would find it funny."

She smelled of bonfire and tasted of strawberries.

"What are you doing?" she asked.

"I'm sorry. I'll never do that again."

"I told you to never knock me off the horse. I didn't tell you not to do what you were doing right now—rather, I posed a simple question."

When their mouths separated again, he said, "You're the most beautiful... anything I've seen in my life."

"And you reek of brandy."

And then all the other pieces of the puzzle faded—the deer, the tower, the vanishing—leaving only the wave of black hair, the eyes, the lips, and the body pressed against his.

3

They rode his mare back to the castle—*she* rode, Shea sitting behind—and slipped into his quarters the way a pair of kids slip out of the house to play a dangerous game.

The sex was violent. She didn't let him kiss her anymore or even help her undress—they tore their clothes off like two fighters at separate corners of the ring, after which she pushed him on his back and thrust her hips into his.

It was a voyeuristic but at the same time strangely intimate experience—the sense of pleasure *being done* to his body, and yet he answered every push, their gazes locked. She closed her eyes only in the end, when something exploded in them both.

Later, lying on her side with her back to him, she said, "I'm not that way. I'm not that way, Shea."

Euphoria sliding into an echo, he studied the *sotto in sù* ceiling, the badly painted plump angel extending an olive branch, in twilight, to a bewildered-looking hunter. He could've asked her to elaborate, but what good would it do? She wasn't like that in the sense that sex with her was normally tender? Or she wasn't likely to sleep with someone while being the lover of another?

He traced with his finger the curve of her hip, and bitterness rose in him—at her, at the duke, at himself: he thought how he envied that stupid angel, how he wished he could live in that painting, too, in the season of sunsets, forever postponing the minute the light would disappear.

She stood, picked up her pants, and peeked inside them. "I think I've got a dandelion in there somewhere."

"You've got one in your hair, too. Let me help you."

"Thanks, I can manage."

She strolled to the wine cabinet; opened it. "You didn't drink all those bottles alone, did you, Shea?"

There would have been something deeply wrong with lying to a woman he'd just slept with. "The boy Daniel has been supplying me."

"Why?"

"Why what—why is he supplying me or why am I drinking alone?"

"Why are you drinking."

Words pushed at his throat, and, unable to contain them, he rose on his elbow and said, "I've destroyed the tower, Lena. Well, not literally, but I helped ruin it. The queen sent me here to make sure it gets built, and I failed. Ruined myself in the process."

Her face was an emotionless mask when she turned to him. "I beg your pardon?"

"The tower will crumble within two months."

And then the mask melted, sunset reverted to dawn: she jumped onto the bed to squeeze him in an embrace. She didn't hold back.

"You're going... to crush... me."

"Sorry."

He sucked in air, her face coming into focus, reddened cheeks, a wide smile— and jealousy prickled him, the fact that, minutes after they'd had sex, something else was the source of that unfiltered joy.

"I had no idea you hated the tower that much."

She squinted at him. "But I showed you the book. I thought that was the reason..."

"It was a very vivid tale, Lena, but no. I came here, I saw problems. I believed I could fix everything, like that." He snapped his fingers. "I didn't take time to truly understand what was happening."

"You mistook me for someone else—I don't read tales, Shea. Problems—I presume Brielle or one of her engineers made an error?"

"It's not my place to tell you."

Relief from admitting everything came and went, leaving in its wake the beginning of the end: until now, he realized, he'd allowed some vestigial hope to linger at the back of his mind. Perhaps he'd waited for a miracle to happen, or for Brielle to find a solution. Now, he'd cast his last stone into the pond and let it drown.

But was that the last stone? a voice whispered in his mind. *Is there a solution, perhaps?*

Lena's smile shrank, but didn't disappear. "I realize it's hard for you, but I can't help myself. I'm happy."

She embraced him again, this time carefully, the way a mother would a child.

He patted her on the back. "I'm sorry that I can't feel the same."

She let him go, stood, and picked up her shirt. "What'll happen to you?"

"Do you care?"

A pause, and then a plain, "Yes."

"Daelyn will either imprison me or send me to my family estate. Permanently."

"Then I'm sorry, too. But I want you to know you've done good. You may not believe in the Mimic Tower, but you must believe in something, no? There are many things in this world we can't explain."

Shea thought back to the deer and said, "For example?"

"Did I tell you why Drakiri won't let strangers into their home?"

"Because most strangers are assholes?"

"Because we don't know where our true home is."

"Last time I checked your homeland was in Pangania—or do you mean it metaphorically?"

"Pangania was a waystation, nothing more."

"So Owenbeg is your *second* asylum? Where are you from then, originally?"

"We have no records of where we really came from, only that we arrived from elsewhere, and letting a new person under your roof is seen, traditionally, like sharing this—a vulnerability."

"You people possess too vivid a shared imagination." When she placed her hand on the doorknob, he said, "I don't want this to be the last time."

"Then start by cleaning out your wine cabinet." She took a step into the corridor and paused. "I'll be leaving Owenbeg sometime in the future. You asked if I care? Here's the real answer: you could join me—if your queen doesn't put you under lock and key."

He remembered the roundabout they'd ridden in the settlement, the world's colors spinning around them, the birds, the smells of autumn.

"I think I'm falling in love with you."

"Be careful, then," she said and closed the door behind her.

Dear sis, my beautiful flower—I think I'll stay quiet for a while. I want to be quiet. Too much has happened, and I don't think I've got the strength to carry on even our

imaginary conversations. Don't be mad at me (I know you can't, the dead are the only ones in this world who are at peace), and I swear I'll talk to you again. I'll become whole again.

Just not now.

4

Shea entered the tavern. Behind the counter, the barkeep poured the last drops of the summer into a beer jug—he must've intended to drink it himself, because the establishment stood otherwise empty save for Shea, a decrepit drunk whistling a snore on the bench next to the coat hanger, and Brielle.

She sat in the corner by a lattice window. The lozenges were red in the center, and the sun filtered through that spot, painting a warm shape on the back of her palms lying on the table. It occurred to Shea how bad it looked, the color of blood on her hands.

He lowered himself opposite. "How are you doing?"

Brielle kept silent.

"I would talk about the weather, but it's agonizingly unremarkable today."

"Cut it." She squinted at him, and it was only then that Shea noticed she had no drink.

"What's going on, Brielle?"

She smiled with only her lips. "Why don't *you* tell me?"

"What about?"

"You promised me two months."

The barkeep swung back his head and poured in the beer.

"I promised *us* two months."

She leaned forward. "You slept with Lena yesterday." *Shit.* "I noticed by accident," she said. "I saw her exit your quarters."

"Has anybody else seen her?"

"One witness isn't enough for you? Do the math, Shea—what happens if I slip a word or two to the duke?"

As though having fulfilled his function, the barkeep lowered the jug on the counter. The drunk stopped snoring, and silence stretched across the hall, too thin, too ready to pop.

"What? Why would you do that? Brielle, what's happening?" He reached for her hand, but she pulled it back.

And, as if to compensate for the loss of intimacy, she leaned forward even closer.

"You've betrayed me, that's what's happening."

"Betrayed you by what, by sleeping with Lena?" *She had a romantic affection for him*, it dawned on Shea, and cold beaded his forehead. How the hell hadn't he noticed it before? Two sharing a secret, only able to confide in one another, a fertile ground for all kinds of feelings...

He cleared his throat. "Listen, I find you attractive, too... But, please don't take it the wrong way, our meetings were only that, meetings—"

Brielle started back like a mechanical toy, studied him with wide-open eyes—and then burst into laughter. The drunk by the coat hanger jolted and sat straight.

"What on Earth are you on about, Shea? I couldn't care less if you found me attractive."

"But I thought you said—"

"I said you have a secret and I know it, just as you know mine. So if you're planning to report everything—"

"Report? To whom?"

She raised her finger, and he looked where she pointed. Through the window, past the triangle rooftops, the castle hill was dark at the base and evening-gold at the top where the walls rose.

"Listen, I give up," Shea said. "I give up. I don't want to play this game anymore. Just say whatever you have to say."

"Look at Kayleigh's wing."

Oh my, she's right, she's absolutely right. The abandoned wing should've been dead, but it wasn't. Shea's old balcony and his old windows—one of them stood open, and he thought he saw a movement behind it.

Brielle said, "Is he here to double-check or to arrest me?"

"He who?"

"You tell me. Another guy from the capital, judging by the accent. Did you tell him all about my mistake? How Brielle screwed up basic calculations?"

Why haven't I seen him? he wanted to ask—but, of course, he already knew the answer. The person he'd seen the most of these days was the village boy with linen sacks full of booze.

"I bumped into him right after the decommissioning," Brielle said. "He was talking to Patrick. Wears black gloves."

...walking into a pocket-size theater, eight or nine rows, six of them empty, lowering himself next to a slender man in black gloves, and—'consider this an opportunity'…

"I haven't reported anything to anyone, Brielle. But I may know the guy. I used to know him."

"I don't believe you."

"You shouldn't. I realize how it looks—I wouldn't believe myself, either."

"If he isn't here because of you, then why?"

"Of that, I've absolutely no idea."

5

The picture carried an almost nostalgic air, the narrow path between the battlements a rivulet of stone flowing from the mass of the old castle. Almost. After all, they'd tried to kill him there, Patrick and the duke—but still, for Shea, the memory of seeing Kayleigh's wing for the first time interlocked with the image of the tower, the feeling of anticipation, the first sign of promise since the moment he'd traded his career for the little pink dress in the airship's shadow.

And now he'd done the same again: destroyed whatever he'd had left on principle.

He squinted: someone was there, at the far end of the path. In darkness, the figure was a writhing grub—he couldn't even guess the height. He dove back under the archway and waited.

The figure assumed form and Patrick shot past him, eyes straight ahead.

What the hell is the duke's military counselor doing in Kayleigh's wing? Consorting with the new tenant?

He held still until the steps died down. Then he followed the narrow path.

The tower's furnace through the embrasures, the staircase leading downward, the corridor with the gas lamps. He hesitated—after all, he had no plan for what would come next—and knocked on the door.

"Come in, Ashcroft," said the familiar voice.

Shea pushed on the doorknob and entered his old room. "How did you know it was me?"

"Easy. You don't knock the way the majordomo knocks—apart from her, two people have reasons to see me at this hour, and one of them just left."

"Hello, Aidan."

It was really him—he stood at the window, looking at something outside, thin, black-gloved fingers between the curtains that dripped evening onto the floor.

"Come in, come in, Shea. Great to see you. Have a drink—the carafe's in the bedroom."

He turned and smiled the way people smile who use courtesy as a tool—earnest at a first glance, but with a whiff of professionalism. Gray eyes scurried across Shea like two spiders, assessing. "Your timing's impeccable—although I honestly can't tell if it's by design. Were you following Patrick?"

Shea kept silent. Slender, taller than average but not too tall, with pleasant features but not beautiful enough to stand out in the crowd, the only distinguishing thing about Aidan was his black gloves. He was someone you felt safe to confess to. Probably would've made a fine priest, too.

"Aren't you going to have that drink?"

"I think I've had enough for today," Shea said.

"Oh yes, I've heard, I've heard."

"You've heard—have you been spying on me?"

The smile retracted halfway, vacating the eyes. "I really hope that's a rhetorical question.

"This place," he continued, "it's beautiful, sure, but it lacks finesse. You can't spy on people—you actually struggle to filter out all the irrelevant parts of their life stories. Why don't you take a sit?"

"Why don't you tell me what Patrick was doing here?"

"Telling me he was going to Duma."

"To Duma—why?"

Aidan pursed his lips in an amused manner. "Because I sent him there?"

"Sent him?"

"Oh, easy. I told him the saboteurs he was looking for were holding a rendezvous in Poltava an hour from now. You know, the village past the border."

Of course. Patrick still believed Duma was behind those gaping mouths in the tower's walls.

"It was poor sportsmanship. I didn't even need to plant evidence. I just mentioned to him the saboteurs would be in Poltava, and he immediately took off."

"What do you want with him?"

Aidan gave him a faraway look, like a chess player who doesn't quite see his opponent because part of him is inside his next move. "We must get rid of him, I'm afraid."

"Are you crazy? For heaven's sake—what's up with people today? I'm not killing anybody, Aidan."

"Then Patrick will kill you."

"He's already tried, and I don't think he would go for it again."

"And that's where you're in error. I *do* know he'd paid someone to assassinate you—but that was a brute from the village, and now he's hired a professional. He's meeting him in two days to pay him off."

"The duke—"

"This time, Patrick isn't acting on the duke's orders. He's *keen.* He wants to make up for his mistake, and you've provided him with the perfect opportunity—I'll bet good money the coroner's report would say, 'died in a state of severe inebriation from choking on his own vomit'."

"I'm not going to kill him," Shea said.

"Then you have two choices: die or leave Patrick to me."

"Why are you doing this? I think *you* think you're helping me—but why?"

Aidan lowered himself into a chair and, with a hint at a smile, nodded toward a couch. "Do take a sit."

"Tell me."

"Let's make a deal, shall we? You ride with me to Poltava, I tell you why I'm here."

"I am not going to kill Patrick."

"Then, I guess we'll see what happens when we get there."

Shea sat. "What *would* happen is, there would be no blood. I'd reason with him. Convince him I'm no threat."

Aidan studied him again. "Still an idealist. Perhaps it's a weakness. Perhaps I've backed the wrong horse."

"Backed the...?"

"I'll explain in an hour, at Poltava."

"Aren't you afraid of causing a diplomatic incident?"

"It's a puny border village. Worst case, we bump into a patrol—and remember, I speak the language, I know how they think."

"That's right—you're Dumish, correct? You mask your accent so well, I forgot that."

"Therein lies the difference between us," Aidan said quietly. "After a decade at the Red Hill, I still don't have the luxury of forgetting. But I digress. We'll tell the sentries we were inebriated and took the wrong road. With you in your current state, we won't even need to do a lot of convincing. I'm more concerned about the goons Patrick will bring with him."

Now there are goons. But a voice inside reminded Shea that Aidan was right. The military counselor *had* tried to kill him. *Why did I assume Patrick would simply accept his failure? Was it the same arrogance that drove me to convince the duke to get rid of the Drakiri devices?*

The room submerged in silence while a thrush somewhere in the courtyard drummed out the minutes.

"Okay," Shea said. "I'll go. But remember: no blood."

"Let's hope Patrick agrees."

At the stables, Aidan simply nodded to the keeper, a fellow with a beard that seemed to have picked up rust from the gate. "Hullo, James."

The man produced a smile so wide one could count all his remaining teeth.

"Just how long have you been here?" Shea whispered.

"For a week," Aidan said. "I found out you'd made friends, and had to work fast."

He selected two horses, a chestnut mare and a beautiful pitch-black stallion.

"This one is the duke's. The name's Onyx. I'm quite fond of him."

6

They followed a creek down the plain, meager hillside covered in bush's bristle to their left, forest to the right. The water was glass, reflecting little but the clean cider sky and the cloud front to the west.

"It's going to rain soon," Shea said. "How do we evade the border sentries?"

"Our friend Patrick is a military counselor, he knows the patrol patterns. We just have to follow him." A wave of the black glove, sweeping three smudged auburn spots at the horizon. Horses. "The difficulty, actually, lies in not being noticed *by them*—at least not until we're deep enough into Duma territory."

"Were you planning on killing him there?"

"Of course. Duma would dispose of the bodies to avoid a diplomatic incident. They'd cover it up for us, Shea." He half-turned in the saddle and produced a smile. "I'm still planning it, you know."

"No. I'll talk to him."

"That would be putting too much faith into your own persuasive abilities. See that you don't learn it the hard way."

The clouds blinked, grunted, prompting a neigh from Shea's mare.

"Easy, girl," He patted her on the neck.

The mare neighed again.

"Calm your animal down, Shea. You don't want them to notice us."

"Easy, girl, easy. There's nothing to be afraid of." *Yet.*

Shea clung to the black mane and shot a glance back: ten miles away now, against the first pale stars, the tower looked like its twin from Lena's folio: no longer a part of the sky but an extension of the earth, as though something immense had tried to get free and pulled up the crust in the process.

He turned and concentrated on what lay ahead.

Aware now of his mare's tendency to voice its discontent, they covered the last quarter mile to Poltava on foot.

First to emerge from the darkness was a rundown fence with three chestnut horses tied to it. Then came a dragon, and another one, and another, wooden figurines straddling the roofs' ridges—or were those logs someone had pulled from a bonfire?

How had the duke put it? See what they've done to the place, see it for yourself. Above Shea's head, thunder rolled like a roly-poly, left to right, right to left, and the rain started, abruptly and in full force, making the houses' burns seem fresh.

For all the talk of Poltava, it was a tiny village, no more than fifty homes—and half of them were coal husks, death on one side of the main street, life on the other.

"Why on earth won't they rebuild those?" Shea said.

"There's a decree prohibiting that."

"Why?"

"So that people will remember."

"My knowledge of history is rusty, but wasn't it Duma that massacred this place?"

Aidan sighed. "This depends on whose account you're inclined to believe."

"The duke thinks so."

"Then it must be true, right? If the duke thinks so."

On the live side, behind the rain torrents, fireflies of windows smoldered.

Shea said, "Where do you suppose Patrick went?"

"Look, Patrick does what Patrick does. He arrives. He intends to find the saboteurs, so what's his best move? To interrogate some locals. They tell him, of course, that they haven't heard of any secret congregation—which is the honest-to-goodness truth. But, knowing Patrick…"

"He would presume they're sheltering the criminals."

"And his next step…?"

"Obviously, to search the houses."

"One, two, three, four." Aidan waved his gloved index finger theatrically, and on the count of four, a door in the middle of the street flew open, letting warm light into the rain's monochrome. Three men stepped outside.

Aidan brushed his wet hair from his forehead. "Patrick! Patrick!"

The tallest silhouette turned like a puppet in a shadow theatre.

"We're here, Patrick."

There was a moment of chaos, voices coughing and barking. Then the figures began toward them.

There it goes. Shea wiped the water from his face. He should've felt adrenaline, revenge's foretaste—but it was all *unclean*, the lead-pregnant clouds, the half-burnt village, even ambushing the man who'd tried to kill him.

"Aidan!" Patrick called out from the rain. "What are you doing here?"

"What does it look like?"

Was he *enjoying it*?

The duke's counselor stopped a few feet away, gray threads stitching the air and turning his face into a featureless mask. Another thing was tangible, though, and crude: the heavy crossbow the fellow to Patrick's left held at the ready.

"Hello, Ashcroft." The voice was featureless, too. "It looks like a setup to me."

Aidan smiled. "We need to talk."

"So, who has whom on the leash? Ashcroft you, or you Ashcroft? I should've known better than to trust a Dumian."

Aidan's smile morphed into a frown—but only for a second. "Nothing wrong with having regrets, Patrick."

"I don't have *regrets*—in case you haven't noticed, there's an arbalest pointed at your smug face."

"For how long, is the question."

Without saying a word, the man with the crossbow stepped through the rain, walked over an invisible line, and froze next to Aidan.

"Colm, what the hell are you doing?"

Aidan whistled. "Oh, the sweet power of gold."

"You're all dead—you too, Colm." Despite his words, Patrick took a step back. "You're still with me, Duane?"

The fellow he'd called Duane visibly hesitated, shifting his weight from one leg to another.

"Duane?"

At that moment, on an impulse, as though observing himself from the outside, Shea said, "Duane isn't an idiot. He knows how unpleasant an injury—any injury—would make his way back to the border."

Did I really say that?

"Duane!"

"Your choice, Duane," Aidan said.

The man shrunk his head into his shoulders, lurched forward. Hurried past them. In a second, his stride went from andante to allegro: he broke into a run.

"Now we can talk odds."

"What Ashcroft said about the injuries —the same applies to you. I don't do surrender."

The rain turned into a drizzle, as abruptly as it had started, revealing Patrick's face, the face of a sad spaniel, the slightly hunched shoulders, bony legs. For the first time, Shea saw him, really saw him.

"I won't hurt you, Patrick."

"Then why are you here?"

"I'm not a threat. I've no idea why you haven't understood it by now. If it's your position at the duke's court you fear for, don't—I couldn't care less."

Patrick studied him and smiled with the corners of his mouth. "You know what I hate the most about you? Your self-righteousness. You capital types, you're infallible, aren't you?"

If only you knew, Shea thought, *if only...*

"You do realize, Ashcroft, that you've said goodbye to your own honor? I want to hear you rationalize this from your moral high ground, luring a man into a trap, bribing his companions."

"*Companion*," said Aidan. "I've only bribed Colm here."

"I'm talking to the intendant guy. How do you rationalize that?"

"How do you rationalize trying to kill me?" Shea asked.

Something changed in Patrick: a wave traveled from his feet through his body, straightening the back, unfurling the shoulders, pushing forward the jaw. "Because you deserve it. You all do. Every single one of you at the Red Hill. You live off of us, and when you make a mistake—no, even when you disregard a direct order from a ruling monarch—you don't really go away, do you? You get another assignment. You come to issue orders to *us*."

"It's your own choice to—" Aidan began.

"And you're how old, Ashcroft—thirty-five?" Patrick squinted. "I'm almost fifty—I've served the duke for the most of my life. I make one mistake, one tiny mistake with you, and that's it."

"You're talking about *my* life here," Shea said.

"*One* mistake. And he tells me he's already preparing a replacement."

The honeycombs of the palace towers, the guy in the orange jacket jumping around the theater stage. *I understand the poor bastard. The man who tried to assassinate me, I know how he feels.* "I didn't choose to come. If I could unburden you—"

"Fuck off!" Patrick spat on the ground. "I didn't get the second chance you got—and I haven't even disobeyed the duke. You're—"

"I'm sorry. Not about the things you've done, but about your situation."

"—bastards. I would choke you all at the Red Hill if I could, even the children, even the children."

He wasn't lying, Shea thought, and it wasn't a hyperbole. Patrick was too simple to put up a facade, and—this much had been clear from their first conversation during the 'reception', back then, in the yellow room—he possessed a large capacity for hatred. *Who knows what his story was; abused as a child? his peers didn't like him enough?*—but there he stood, in his current state, hating himself and, by extension, the universe.

And sometimes, the universe obliged hate with a target.

"Hand me the crossbow," Shea said to the guy—what was his name? Colm?

The black glove patted him on the shoulder. "Glad to see you've finally come to your senses."

Shea raised the weapon and aimed it at Patrick's face. "Walk."

"What?"

"Walk. Turn around and walk. Down the street, to the end of it, out of my sight."

Patrick pursed his lips. Took a few steps backward. Turned.

As he moved away—from them and from the border—the sky cleared up, the stars brighter and closer now. Under their light, the tall figure receded between the mangled houses and the whole ones. He glanced back only once, at the very end of the street, the hunched shoulders, the spaniel face, barely discernable now.

Then he disappeared into a foreign land.

"This was a mistake. You're banking too much on patrols stumbling upon him," Aidan said. "My decision to support you—"

"What the hell do you mean?" Shea hurled the crossbow into the mud. "What are you talking about? Tell me at last why you're here."

"Let Colm go."

"I don't care—he can go."

Without a word, the man who'd betrayed Patrick turned and left.

"I'm here because you have the keys to my future."

Shea chuckled. Somewhere in his belly, laughter uncurled, growing, working its way up. "What future? Look at me."

"I'm looking. I—"

"Look at me!" He shook his hands, palms up. "What future? Where? I've been exiled. Reduced to nothing."

"You still think of this as an *exile*? Did you not hear anything I said to you back then, at the theater?"

"*Consider this a wonderful opportunity*—oh yes, what a mockery."

"Mockery? Listen, Daelyn has sent three people to the provinces. The intendancy system is brand new. She wants to see which one of you can control the local lords better."

The tingles crawled up to his throat, making Shea giggle.

Aidan scowled. "What's wrong with you? Owenbeg's the most important assignment of the three, for obvious reasons. The tower. Queen was impressed with your defiance, heaven knows why, when you spared those protesters. I guess the last time someone defied her was decades ago. Hey, are you listening? Do you understand what I'm saying to you? Daelyn is grooming her potential successors."

Laughter bent Shea in two, his knees sinking into the brown mash.

"What in the... We don't have time for this, Shea. I'm here to help you."

He managed to slip a word between bursts: "Why?"

"Damn it, stand up. Because, to quote you from a minute ago—look at me. I'm Duma. I'll always remain Duma. Remember what Patrick just said, that one should never trust a Dumian? Remember what you yourself said about my accent? I'm an émigré, and that's my ceiling. But with you, I'll rise. *We'll* rise. We've taken care of Patrick. We'll take care of the duke, if needed. We just need to get the bloody tower done."

And then the dam broke, everything Shea had been trying to lock away burst free, poured out of him in a soup of sobs and laughter.

"Have you gone mad? Stand up!"

"I can't." Shea stared at his palms. "I can't. I've destroyed it."

There is a solution, a voice whispered in his mind. The solution came clearly. It lay in the part of his past he'd tried his best to bury, in the room with soot stains and in the abandoned cellar underneath the rosewood trapdoor. *No*, he thought, trying to block out the image.

"Destroyed what, damn it? Destroyed what?"

"The tower." He raised his eyes at Aidan. "It was held together by the Drakiri devices. I had them taken out."

"What? Hey, hey, listen to me. Shea? Listen to me! Whatever you've done to the tower, you need to put it back together, do you understand? Do you understand? Do you realize what depends on it?"

"I can't. The duke destroyed the devices."

But you know the solution, the voice whispered, and in his mind's eye, the rosewood trapdoor opened and he stepped into the cellar filled with purple glow, filled with objects he thought of as 'tulips' because someone else, someone he used to know had called them that, in the cellar beneath the ruined workshop, beneath the room with soot stains.

No, he thought, *no, I won't return there, I won't*—but deep inside, a part of him that had been weighing the possibilities considered the scales.

And he knew in whose favor they were tipped.

7

The girl had opened the door for him, and the dance hall's golden lights momentarily blinded him.

Shea didn't know her name—she was, after all, just an attendant—but to him, she'd been all the gloss of the capital: blond hair coiled into an elaborate braid, kohl-lined almond eyes, naked forearms.

"First night at the Red Hill?" She gave him a perfect smile.

"Is it that obvious?" he said and added, clumsily, "It's all I've ever dreamt of."

"You'll get used to it. Don't worry— everyone does. You'll be fine."

He'd never learned her name, never seen her again—but that moment stayed with him when she'd patted him on the shoulder, nudging him into the hall, toward the golden lights, toward all the beautiful people swirling in a waltz.

At the rain-whipped street, on his knees, he remembered the kohl-lined eyes which looked at him, as if saying: *you could have it all back. You could have it all, and more.*

See Yaroslav Barsukov's story "Tower of Mud and Straw II: The Adversary" online at Metaphorosis.
If you liked it, leave a comment. Authors love that!
Remember to subscribe to our e-mail updates so you'll know when new stories are posted.

Copyright

Title information

Metaphorosis October 2020

ISSN: 2573-136X (online)
ISBN: 978-1-64076-179-7 (e-book)
ISBN: 978-1-64076-180-3 (paperback)

Copyright

Publisher

Metaphorosis

a magazine of speculative fiction

Metaphorosis Magazine is an imprint of
Metaphorosis Publishing
Neskowin, OR, USA

www.metaphorosis.com

"Metaphorosis" is a registered trademark.

Discounts available

Substantial discounts are available for educational institutions, including writing workshops. Discounts are also available for quantity purchases. For details, contact Metaphorosis at metaphorosis.com/about

Metaphorosis Publishing

Metaphorosis offers beautifully written science fiction and fantasy. Our imprints include:

Metaphorosis Magazine
Plant Based Press
Verdage

You can also find us:
@MetaphorosisMag, @MetaphorosisRev,
@Metaphorosis
www.facebook.com/metaphorosis

Help keep Metaphorosis running by supporting us at
Patreon.com/metaphorosis

See more about some of our books on the following pages.

Metaphorosis Magazine

Metaphorosis

a magazine of speculative fiction

Metaphorosis is an online speculative fiction magazine dedicated to quality writing. We publish an original story every week, along with author bios, interviews, and notes on story origins.

We also publish monthly print and e-book issues, as well as yearly Best of and Complete anthologies.

Come and see us online at magazine.Metaphorosis.com

Metaphorosis: Best of 2019

The best science fiction and fantasy stories from *Metaphorosis* magazine's fourth year.

Metaphorosis 2019

All the stories from *Metaphorosis* magazine's fourth year. Fifty-two great SFF stories.

Metaphorosis:
Best of 2018

The best science fiction and fantasy stories from *Metaphorosis* magazine's third year.

Metaphorosis
2018

All the stories from *Metaphorosis* magazine's third year. Fifty-two great SFF stories.

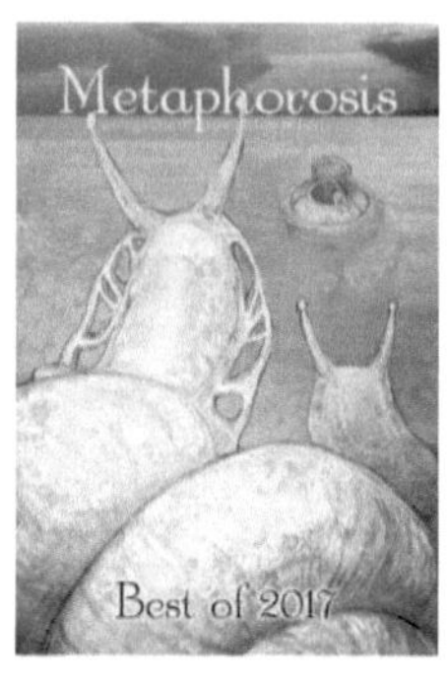

Metaphorosis:
Best of 2017

The best science fiction and fantasy stories from *Metaphorosis* magazine's *second* year.

Metaphorosis
2017

All the stories from *Metaphorosis* magazine's second year. Fifty-three great SFF stories.

Metaphorosis: Best of 2016

The best science fiction and fantasy stories from *Metaphorosis* magazine's first year.

Metaphorosis 2016

Almost all the stories from *Metaphorosis* magazine's first year.

Plant Based Press

Vegan-friendly science fiction and fantasy, including an annual anthology of the year's best SFF stories.

Best Vegan SFF of 2019

The best vegan-friendly science fiction and fantasy stories of 2019!

Best Vegan SFF of 2018

The best vegan-friendly science fiction and fantasy stories of 2018!

Best Vegan SFF of 2017

The best vegan-friendly science fiction and fantasy stories of 2017!

Best Vegan SFF of 2016

The best vegan-friendly science fiction and fantasy stories of 2016!

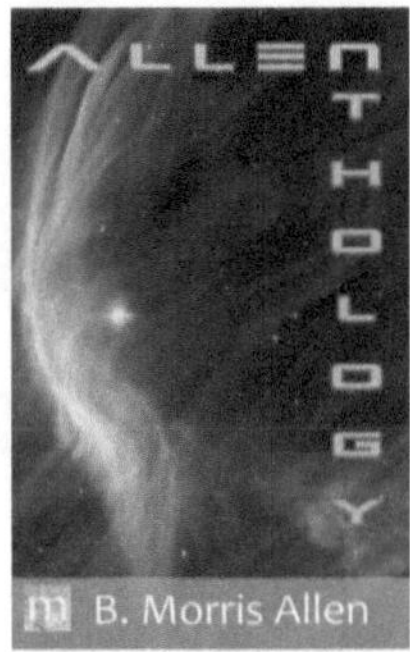

Susurrus

A darkly romantic story of magic, love, and suffering.

Allenthology: Volume I

A quarter century of SFF, including the full contents of the collections *Tocsin, Start with Stones,* and *Metaphorosis.*

Verdage

Science fiction and fantasy books for writers – full of great stories, often with an additional focus on the craft of speculative fiction writing.

Reading 5X5 x2

Duets

How do authors' voices change when they collaborate?

A round-robin of five talented science fiction and fantasy authors collaborating with each other and writing solo.

Including stories by Evan Marcroft, David Gallay, J. Tynan Burke, L'Erin Ogle, and Douglas Anstruther.

Score

an SFF symphony

What if stories were written like music? *Score* is an anthology of varied stories arranged to follow an emotional score from the heights of joy to the depths of despair – but always with a little hope shining through.

Reading 5X5	**Reading 5X5**
Five stories, five times	*Writers' Edition*
Twenty-five SFF authors, five base stories, five versions of each – see how different writers take on the same material.	Two extra stories, the story seed, and authors' notes on writing. Over 100 pages of additional material specifically aimed at writers.

www.ingramcontent.com/pod-product-compliance
Lightning Source LLC
Chambersburg PA
CBHW020329110726
47898CB00003B/809